VICTORIA II

Daniel A. Willis

D. X. Varos

Published by:
D. X. Varos, Ltd
7665 E. Eastman Ave. #B101
Denver, CO 80231

Book cover design and layout by, Ellie Bockert Augsburger of
Creative Digital Studios.
www.CreativeDigitalStudios.com
Cover design features:
White silk fabric By Stillfx / Adobe Stock
royal red velvet pillow on white background By Dmitry
Koksharov / Adobe Stock

ISBN
978-1-941072-91-2 (paperback)
978-1-941072-92-9 (ebook)

INTRODUCTION

Alternative history, otherwise known as the world of "what if," has held the fascination of many an author. Perhaps we all have experienced episodes in life that have left us wondering how we would have fared if it had gone so very differently.

This story asks that very question, but on a more global scale. People of the 21st century tend to discount our modern-day royals and the effect the have on the course of history, or the future. They do so at their own peril.

As we will soon see, an inopportune premature death will have a farther reach than any could have imaged in the mid-1800s. But to fully understand the ramifications of what seems to have been a minor event on the world stage, let us first quickly review the history as we have come to know it.

Queen Victoria of the United Kingdom and her Prince Consort, Prince Albert, had nine children. What is most important for our story, is not the number, but which came first. Under the rules of succession in force in Victoria's time, a brother always came before his sister regardless of who is older. This was how Victoria came to the Throne to begin with, she was her father's only child, so had no brother to supplant her.

In the case of Victoria and Albert, their first child was a daughter, also named Victoria, and always called Vicky within the family. She was followed by a brother, Albert Edward, called Bertie by his parents, and later King Edward VII by the world. There were seven more siblings whose descendants went on to sit upon most of the thrones of Europe. Even in today's world of only ten remaining European monarchies, Queen Victoria's descendants reign over five of them.

One of the most notable descendants was the eldest child of Princess Vicky. Vicky was allowed to marry for love, but her parents stacked the deck to encourage her to fall in love with the future King of Prussia. She took the bait and ended up married to Prince Fritz, ultimately finding herself styled as the German Empress. In due course, her son succeeded his father and became known to history as Kaiser Wilhelm II, one of the leading figures of World War I, in fact, its leading instigator.

But what if Vicky had no younger siblings? Then she would have been her mother's heiress. As such, she never would have been allowed to marry the ruler of a foreign country. Likely, a younger son of a large family of princes would have been found for her, and he would serve as her Prince-Consort, just her father had done for her mother.

But then what happens to Kaiser Bill? Simple, he was never born. Then, like the falling of dominoes in a row, each missing event triggers another to disappear, and another. We watch history unravel, and rethread itself into a new, unrecognizable cord of rope. And, yet there might still be a stray string here or there that has a vague familiarity to it, like Deja vu.

So now, please read along as we play God and rewrite history.

PROLOGUE

The Duchess of Buccleuch
Mistress of the Robes
Buckingham Palace
2 June 1842

Lady Georgiana Balfour
Balbirnie House
Fife

My Darling Niece,

How very kind of you to think of my well-being during this national tragedy. Yes, let me assure you right off that I am quite unharmed. I had the misfortune to not be in the same carriage with the Queen that morning as we all returned from services at St. James' Chapel. She wanted to ride alone with the Prince; this was a common request of hers. She liked showing to all who cared to look, how much she was in love with her husband, and he with her. After two decades of rule under her lascivious uncles, she believes the people are ready for purity and marital devotion from their Sovereign.

I call my placement in the second carriage "misfortune" for I was forced to witness those horrible events unfold without being able to do anything to prevent them. At first, I thought Providence had spared all because that madman's pistol seemed to be jammed. But then, he was able to re-cock the firing mechanism and it fired quite unexpectedly, knocking him to the ground. The shot, having gone off without being aimed, missed the Queen entirely, yet caused more damage than if it had struck her. It found a new mark, in the side of the Prince's head. The doctors assured Her Majesty he never felt pain. They are of the opinion he was already dead by the time he landed in her lap.

I am sorry to weigh you down with such unpleasantness, but you are no longer a child, now a wife and mother yourself. (By the way, I think Emily is a beautiful name!) I tell you these things not as an aunt, but as your oldest and dearest friend who so needs that friendship to bolster me now. After all, I am only a few years older than you, and I truly need someone to confide in about my concerns. The other ladies here are all Whig wives and daughters and treat me as the outsider because the Queen chose to keep me on after the government changed. Me, who outranks all of them! And let's not forget that if Charles II had married his first mistress, as old Monmouth always claimed, *I* would be the Queen now, and then we'd see who was on the outside! But I digress.

Because the Queen has entrusted me with her friendship as well as her favor, it is up to me to try to see her through these dark times. It was no secret the Queen was with child, stress on the "was." She miscarried within hours following the shooting. What has not been made public is that Dr. Clark does not hold out much hope that she will be able to carry another child to term.

Not that it much matters. It is hard to imagine she would ever consent to marry again. Once losing a love so all-consuming as that she had with the Prince, I cannot see a path that would lead her back to matrimony.

Now, the future will rest on those chubby little shoulders of the Princess Victoria Adelaide, and she just barely a year and a half. The poor dear will never know her father. Yet, I somehow feel the Queen will never let him go. She has already ordered his rooms to continue to be made up as if he will come in at any time. And she will not allow anyone to speak to her of the funeral arrangements. The Prime Minister has had to step in and make them with the help of the Duchess of Kent. She was the Prince's aunt as well as his mother-in-law, you know. It now falls to me to try to prepare the Queen for the funeral, a task I cannot fail at, but one I am truly dreading. Her mind has been pushed to its limits. I am unsure of her ability to get through this.

Oh, my dearest Georgie, I am sorry to burden you with such distressing words. But getting them out on paper has already helped me more than I can express. And I know I can count on your discretion by not repeating my remarks about Her Majesty's state of mind. As you have always been there for me, and I for you, I remain your devoted auntie and friend,

CHAPTER 1
July 1857

"Are you sure you have packed everything we will need?"

"Yes, Vicky, for the forty-seventh time."

"Oh, Louie, don't exaggerate. I'm sure it has not been more than twenty," Vicky teased. "But I can't help it. Finally, my first trip on my own, and overseas to boot!" Princess Victoria Adelaide, known universally as Vicky by those who knew her personally, and as the Princess Royal to those who didn't, was likely the most talked-about teenager in the world, but had not yet seen any of it.

"If you count barely going across the Channel as 'overseas' and being constantly scrutinized by the watchful eyes of the Princess of Hohenlohe, the King of Belgium, and the Grand Duchess of Mecklenburg, who all have strict orders from your mother to ensure you behave yourself, as 'being on your own'" replied Louie, the nickname of Lady Louisa Howard, Vicky's only close friend.

Vicky, being only sixteen, would not technically have her own ladies-in-waiting until she reached her majority late next year. However, Louie, the youngest of her mother's allotment, had effectively filled the role since arriving at Court a year ago. While most of the Queen's ladies came and went as the government changed, Louie was there as a personal favor to her aunt, one the Queen's few personal friends, the Duchess of Sutherland. It was the Duchess who suggested that the then-fifteen-year-old princess needed someone whose duties were exclusively to take care of her, and that her niece, who was two years older than Vicky, was perfect for the job.

Not even the wise Duchess could have foreseen how close the two girls would become. While publicly, they were princess and servant, behind closed doors they were thick of thieves. Here, in the privacy of Vicky's bedroom at Buckingham Palace, they dropped all formality and titles, and were simply Vicky and Louie.

The age different between the girls was not even noticeable. Vicky had always been a bright child and was considered to be more mature than her tender age would otherwise suggest. Most contributed this to being her mother's daughter, and therefore she had to grow up rather fast by necessity. But, as the Queen often pointed out, Vicky was also her father's daughter, and shared his love of all things mechanical and scientific.

"I don't care if it's across the Channel or an ocean. It is to a land not ruled by my mother, so that makes it officially a foreign trip abroad," Vicky declared, while tying the third bonnet she had tried on. This one was pale blue and best matched the deeper azure shades of the overcoat she decided to where while traveling.

"Speaking of the Queen, you are about one hallway away from being late. You best get moving," Louise pointed out. "I'll take care of the luggage while you say your goodbyes." She waited until Vicky half-trotted down the hall before signaling for the footmen standing at the corner by the stairs to gather the troops to begin the arduous task moving a princess' belongings for her journey. Looking at the mountain of suitcases and garment bags, Louie motioned to the first footman in the door. "Lucky for you it's only a four-day trip. Any longer, this might have started looking like hard work."

***

Vicky knocked twice before entering her mother's office/study. Queen Victoria of the United Kingdom of Great Britain and Ireland and her Colonies Beyond the Seas, Defender of the Faith stood staring out the window, looking more pensive that usual. A small woman of only five feet tall, she almost looked like a child dressed for a funeral in her ever-present widow weeds. Today her hair was adorned with a white lace veil tied underneath to pull its weight off her neck on this warm summer day. Still a young woman, not even forty yet, she retained her beauty, even if mixed with a large dose of melancholy.

After a quick curtsey, "Mama?" Vicky tried to reach through the sense of dread that nearly always surrounded her mother.

The Queen turned and made an effort at half a smile. "Is everything prepared then?"

"Yes, I am ready to go to the train station. Are you sure you won't come to see me off? It's a beautiful day, and it would do you a world of good to go out in it. It would also do the people a bit of good to see their queen."

"Oh Vicky, you know I can't, and you know why I can't. Why must you harp on so?"

"Not harping, just pointing out how lovely the summer day it is."

"Sweetheart, I know you mean well. I'm afraid I would not be good company today anyhow. Now that it is time to say good-bye, I suddenly don't want to. Would you hate me if I changed my mind and sent one of your Cambridge cousins instead?" the older Victoria asked in an almost hopeful voice.

"Mama, I could never hate you. But I would be very cross with you after I have been packing for three days."

"Well, okay, I guess we can't have that," the Queen said reluctantly. "But I'm so afraid for you. You'll be exposed to sorts of dangers."

"I'm going to a wedding, not into a war zone."

"With those Habsburgs, you can never be quite sure," Victoria quipped.

Vicky laughed and was happy her mother could still try to crack a joke. "Don't worry, Mama. I'll be surrounded by family, most of whom you've ordered to spy on me, I'm told by the way. The only danger I'll be in is staying out of Cousin Hanover's way."

"Don't mock the less fortunate, Vicky. It's not Georgie's fault he's blind. He's just another victim, like the rest us, of this family's curse. It really is a pity Uncle Cumberland had no other children. It seems almost unfair to force someone in Georgie's condition to be king."

12

"We are not cursed. What happened to Papa was of course tragic, but it was one incident, not a curse." Vicky admonished.

"He would be so proud of you today, almost grown up, going on you first foreign mission." the Queen looked as if she might begin to cry.

"It's a wedding, Mama, not a mission. It's a happy occasion that family should be together for. And don't forget it's as much as Coburg wedding as it is a Habsburg one. Uncle Leopold has seen to that by inviting every shirt-tail cousin he could find."

"Tell that to Emperor Franz Joseph." Victoria rolled her eyes. "And trust me, our side of the family will be heavily outnumbered. There are dozens of Habsburgs running around Europe and dwindling few Coburgs."

"Yes, but Uncle Leopold has sons and grandsons, and there is still Uncle August's children and grandchildren."

"But they are all Catholics now. Once Uncle Ernie is gone, that will be the last of the Protestant line, save you my darling child. And someday you will marry and no longer be a Coburg yourself."

"Someday ..." Vicky repeated.

"But no husband shopping for you on this trip, young lady," the Queen suddenly snapped out of nostalgia. "All of the men there will be Catholic, and of course you cannot marry any of them. This brings me to another important point. There is a lot of evil in the world Vicky, like the kind of evil that took your blessed Papa from us. So, not only as your mother, but also as your queen looking after the only British heir I have, I cannot allow you to travel willy-nilly about the Continent unprotected."

"But Mama, we have been through this. I will have Louie with me at all times as a chaperone, and beyond that, I will be with cousins the entire time I am in Brussels."

"But you have to *get* to Brussels first. Therefore, I am assigning you a bodyguard."

"Mama, that is not necessary."

"I say it is, and what I say is what matters." The Queen then rang a bell from her desk, which Vicky knew would summon the Private Secretary, whose office was just outside the one they stood in. Had she not entered thru a side door reserved for family, she would have walked right past him.

With two knocks, Charles Grey stepped into the doorway and bowed his head. "Yes, Ma'am?'

"Send in Lt. Saint Albans, Charles."

"Very good, Ma'am." Grey backed out of the door and was replaced in moment by a young man in military uniform, who saluted smartly before entering.

Vicky was immediately taken aback by both the lieutenant's apparent youth and his handsomeness. He could have been no older than she was, with a beautifully shaped face, topped by a standard military cut to his sandy-colored hair. Dressed in the uniform of the Yeoman Guard, its red buttonless overcoat only accentuated the young man's broad chest, while the knee-breeches showcased his well-shaped legs.

"Vicky, may I present the Duke of Saint Albans. He is a member of the corps of my personal guard. Lt. Saint Albans, as you have been instructed, you will be

14

protecting my daughter, the Princess Royal, during her travels to Brussels."

"Yes, Your Majesty," Saint Albans said, maintaining his military "at attention" position and not looking at the Queen as she spoke.

"You are to be at her side at all times. You will be traveling also with a lady-in-waiting, Lady Louisa Howard, who will attend the princess during her intimate needs, and while she sleeps. But all other times, her safety is in your hands, and on your head." The Queen added the last bit with more than a hint of warning in her voice.

"Understood, Ma'am."

"Very well, I am sure your commander has given you all of your more specific instructions. You may wait for the princess at her coach."

"Yes, Ma'am." Saint Albans saluted again and walked backwards out of the royal presence, not turning around until he reached the door.

"I do hope he can overcome your objections. I purposely selected someone close to your age, but yet someone who has had a least a year of training in the protective service. As you will be spending a good deal of time with him, I do hope his age, and the fact that he is of the higher ranks of my Peerage, will give the two of you something to talk about during the trip."

"I have no doubt Louie will find *something* to talk about with such a handsome young man," Vicky giggled.

"Now Vicky, go and have a good time. But remember, this is not just a family wedding. You are also representing your country there and me personally. So, be on your best behavior."

"Of course, Mama."

CHAPTER 2

During the train ride to the coastal town of Folkstone, Vicky allowed her inner child to show. She exclaimed with delight at each new image from the train windows. Having never left the capital, except to go on holiday at Windsor, she was fascinated by the wide openness of the farmlands. When the English Channel came into view, all she could do is stare in awe.

The trio of travelers, Vicky, Louie, and Lt. Saint Albans, road in the royal rail car purchased by the government to be used by a queen who rarely traveled anywhere. She only used it to go to Windsor twice a year, once in August to escape the heat of the city and again in December to celebrate the holidays with Vicky and any relatives who might be visiting from abroad.

Between bouts of pointing out the window yelling "look at that," Vicky tried to carry on a conversation with her newly-assigned bodyguard.

"If I remember my family history correctly, you are one of the dukes who are directly descended from King Charles II," Vicky used as an opening comment.

"That's correct. There's me, and the Dukes of Buccleuch, Grafton, and Richmond. Each of our ancestors were sons of the Merry Monarch by a different mistress," he answered, obviously rather proud of his royal heritage.

"Which mistress was yours?" Louie asked.

"Well, milady, I don't have any mistresses," he answered sheepishly. "But my many times great-grandmother was Nell Gwyn, the actress."

"I recall a funny story about how her son got the Saint Albans title," Vicky said.

"There have been a few good ones circulated about," he said.

"The one I heard was that she held her son out the window protesting that the King had not given him a title. When King Charles saw his son from below, dangling precariously over the courtyard, he cried out 'God save the Duke of Saint Albans!'" which set both girls giggling at the thought.

"That's the cleaner version, to be sure," Saint Albans responded.

"Oh?" Vicky asked, her curiosity peaked. "What's the other one."

"It is not appropriate for fine young ladies, is what that is," he blushed.

"Then we shall be careful not to repeat it to any," Vicky giggled some more.

"Vicky!" Louie exclaimed in mock shock.

"Oh Louie, if I am to be queen one day, I should know all about my nobles, should I not? Go on, Lieutenant, tell us the story."

He looked at Louie, as if for permission, she nodded her head slightly. "Well, Sweet Nell, she was

18

known for her bawdy mannerisms and language. On one occasion when the King paid her a visit, he asked after their son. She called into the other room, 'Come here you little bastard, your father wants to see you.' When the king admonished her for her language, she protested, 'I have no other name to call him.' Charles got the hint and shortly after the little boy got his title."

Vicky blushed but laughed heartily at the story. "That is quite funny. I wish we had colorful people like that around court now. It feels more like a wake there all the time rather the seat of the kingdom."

"Surely it's not as bad as all that, Your Highness" the lieutenant said.

"It is. Mother frowns upon any merriment around her. And, when we are alone like this, please call me Vicky. Everyone else does. And what can I call you? Lt. Saint Albans is a bit of a mouthful."

"My given name is William, but all of my friends call me Billy."

"Well, if we are not friends yet, I certainly hope we will be by the time we are returning home. So Billy it is."

"And everyone calls me Louie," Lady Louisa spoke up, trying to be part of the conversation.

"It is a pleasure to be *in*formally introduced to you both." Billy responded diplomatically, though not taking his eyes off Vicky.

As the train rolled along the three continued in congenial conversation getting to know each other until they reached the port town of Folkstone, where the royal party would transfer to a waiting ferry on which to cross the channel.

Prior to this day, Vicky had never traveled anywhere but Windsor Castle, during which sojourns she was with her mother and the well-wishers would line the roads to the train station in London, and again along the Great Hill up to the castle in Windsor. During these trips she tried to smile and wave at the people lining the streets. Her mother's fear of assassins always kept them in a closed carriage, but Vicky always sat with her face close to the windows so she could feel at least a little closer to the people.

Here, at the Folkstone train station, she saw the small crowd of people that had gathered and thought nothing of it. The local constabulary kept them a respectable distance from the train and from the landau waiting to take Vicky and her companions to their boat.

It was only after she stepped from the royal car, that she noticed this crowd was different than she had ever experienced in London and Windsor. There were no applause as she appeared. There were no cheers. *Oh my goodness*, she thought, *they don't know who I am. But then why would they? They have never seen me.*

In an effort to introduce herself as their princess, she started waving at them with the regal wave as taught by her governess several years previously. As she did this, Louise and Billy left the royal car behind and the attendant closed the door.

Upon seeing the door of the royal car close, one man yelled from the crowd, "Where's the Queen?" He was quickly followed by others quickly calling out "We want to see our queen!" "Do we even have a queen anymore?" "Has anyone seen the queen?" and so forth.

Vicky, not sure what to do, noticed that was a little elevated dais at the end of the platform. Given its position right next to the engine, she surmised it must be for the conductor to use to leave the train while it's in the station. She moved towards the platform, not really sure what she was going to do. Her thought was if the crowd could only see that a member of the royal family was indeed there, maybe that would calm them down.

Billy, not liking the look of the crowd as they seemed to be angrier the longer they stood asking for the queen, caught up to Vicky, seeing she intended to go up to the platform. "You Royal Highness," he said quietly enough not be heard by the on-lookers, "I don't think this is a good idea. You have no idea what is on these people's mind."

"It will be okay. They simply do not understand that I am here in my mother's place. Don't worry, they won't harm me," she assured him, hoping she sounded more convinced than she felt.

Taking a deep breath, she climbed the few steps on to the platform. "Good people," she called out. Her voice faltered a little and did not carry over the din. Those closest seemed to settle a little as they expected her to say something else. Clearing her throat a bit, she called out, more strongly this time, "Good People!" This time her voice was true and strong, the chanting stopped, though no one seemed to know what was going on.

"I am so sorry if you were informed my mother would be here today," Vicky called out to mild grumbling in the crowd. "As that was never the plan, I assure you it is no more than miscommunication." The grumbling grew a bit louder. Vicky's nerves were starting to give way. Out of the corner of eye, she noticed Billy had inched his way to a place just behind her, on the next step down off of the platform. He looked ready to whisk her away at the first sign of anyone attempting to approach the makeshift stage.

"However," Vicky continued speaking more loudly over the continued murmurings, "I am proud to represent Her Majesty on this voyage to celebrate the marriage of our beloved cousin, Princess Charlotte of Belgium." She noticed the crowd quieted considerably. "As I am sure you all know, the Queen, my mother, has many responsibilities. Since the death of my beloved father, she has had to carry that burden alone." Now she saw a few nods from the crowd, especially from some of the women. Perhaps they were widows themselves who had to carry on alone. Then an idea struck Vicky.

"The good news, my fellow Englishmen, is that I am rapidly approaching an age where I can help." This brought the first of a smattering of polite applause. "With this, my first official engagement on behalf of the Crown, I pledge to you that I will spend every day of my life being of service to Her Majesty, to my country, and to you, our loyal subjects." The polite applause rose as she spoke. When she finished she was met with genuine cheers of enthusiasm. To this she smiled and waved to the whole crowd for a few minutes before turning and taking the hand of her young bodyguard to assist her down the few steps.

But it was only once they were in the landau and heading away from the train station, that the duke relaxed. This did not mean his eyes did not continue to dart everywhere looking for more threats.

***

John Stockley left Folkstone station just as the princess finished her little speech. He was disgusted by the fickleness of the crowd. They were there to protest the monarchy, but the little princess had them eating out of her royally gloved hand. Sycophants, the lot of them!

They were not his true compatriots. But that was okay. He knew where to find men of sterner stuff when the time was right. This was just a little event that fell into his lap.

John didn't really think the queen herself would be there. If she left the palace at all, it would have only been to see her daughter off at the station in London. He was pretty sure she would not have accompanied her to the coast.

But the crowd was convinced the senior Victoria was on her way. They managed to rub off on him a little and get his hopes up. He should have known better. "That's okay, she'll be coming out of that pile of bricks soon enough. I'll get my chance then," he thought as he caressed the butt of the pistol in the waistband of his trousers.

CHAPTER 3

"The Prime Minister and the Home Secretary, Ma'am." Charles Grey announced. The two men entered, bowed quickly and advanced towards the queen's desk.

"Lord Palmerston, I was not expecting you today." Victoria didn't bother to hide the annoyance in her voice. Even on their scheduled appointments, she found her Prime Minister tiresome, at best, often devolving into difficult.

"Forgive this sudden intrusion, Your Majesty, but Sir George has received some troubling news which I thought should be brought to your attention immediately," the P.M. responded referring to his companion, Sir George Grey.

"Well Sir George?" the queen prompted.

"Your Majesty, for a few years now, we have been observing larger and more intense republican demonstrations here in the capital. We have been successful keeping the rabble away from the palace so not upset you or your daughter. But today, there was an incident, a small incident to be sure," Grey was quick to add, "but it was outside of London."

"Go on, where was this new incident as you called it?"

"A small crowd of protesters met the princess' train at the coast, Ma'am."

"Is Vicky all right?" sudden concern for her daughter now evident not only in Victoria's voice, but also on her face.

"She is fine, Ma'am. If fact, she handled the situation superbly. Young Saint Albans was never more than arm's length from her, and we had a full complement of guards in the adjacent car to hers, as extra security if needed. Fortunately, they were not. I doubt she was even aware they were there."

Victoria let out a sigh of relief. "I appreciate your discretion in that regard, Sir George. What became of this crowd?"

"After the princess was safely away from the station, my men rounded up the agitators and questioned them. It appears they were all of the opinion that, since you did not accompany the princess, you are ... um ... unwell, Ma'am."

"Unwell?"

"Yes, Ma'am. There were variations to the story, but the similar portions were that you have succumbed to the maladies that afflicted your poor grandfather."

"My people think I have gone mad?" Victoria exclaimed in disbelief.

"Not on the whole, but there are murmurings that are starting to get louder. Of course, we have sat firmly on the papers, so they don't dare repeat such rubbish." Grey suddenly felt the soft touch of Palmerston on his sleeve, cautioning him to not over-excite the Queen.

After a second, he collected himself. "But word of mouth is causing us some concern, Ma'am."

"I see," Victoria looked slightly away from the men, towards the corner of the room. This was her trick of getting them to stop talking and letting her think for a moment. Finally, "and what do you suggest be done about these rumors? Since you seem to have such a tight leash on the press, Sir George, could you not simply make a statement that we have just met and that I, other than missing my daughter terribly, and in excellent spirits?"

It was Palmerston who responded. "I'm afraid that might come off a little contrived, Ma'am. I don't believe it would convince the instigators of such rumors. I suggest you reconsider what I have been suggesting for the past three years as your Prime Minister and the previous three I served as your Home Secretary."

"What? Parade myself through the streets like a common prostitute, or worse, an actress, begging for the attentions of my own people? I think not." Victoria said most firmly, speaking loudly, but not quite yelling.

'But Your Majesty..." Sir George started, Palmerston attempting to stop him. "I beg of you not to underestimate the desire, and the gaining popularity, of republicanism. By secluding yourself away your people, you only incite them."

"That will be enough!" now Victoria was yelling. "Gentlemen. You may withdraw!" she ordered, which was the royal equivalent of saying "Get out!"

The two men, knowing they had been given their marching orders, could do nothing but bow curtly, and leave. Once a safe enough distance down the hall to speak again, Palmerston exclaimed, "What to do with that woman? How do I make her understand her behavior is threatening her own throne?"

"Yes, Henry, the direct approach will get us nowhere. But the reports from Folkstone have opened a possible new avenue to explore." Sir George responded as he admired a portrait of the Princess Royal made for her last birthday.

"That could really be playing with fire, George."

***

Victoria took a moment to compose herself, and to lower her temper. She sat back at her desk and arranged some of her papers, allowing the fever of anger to flow from her. Finally, when she felt calm enough, she rang the bell on her desk.

"Yes, Ma'am?" Charles poked his head in the door.

"Please come in, Charles," the queen invited. The private secretary did so and stood expectantly before her desk. "The Home Secretary has the same surname as you, is he a close relative?"

"He is my cousin, Ma'am. Our fathers were brothers," Charles answered.

"Of course, I should have remembered that. Your grandfather had so many sons, it is rather difficult to remember who is whom."

"Do not concern yourself, Ma'am. My mother has the same problem."

"What do you know of Sir George's personality, Charles?"

"We were raised together as we are nearly the same age, then separated in our teens as he went onto university and I joined the service. But I have always found him a capable man, and quite astute."

"Would you consider him prone to conspiratorial thoughts?"

"Actually, quite the opposite, Ma'am. I have always found him to be very level-headed and a good judge of whatever situation he is in. May I ask why you are inquiring?"

"He seems of the opinion that there is some great republican plot afoot. He has even suggested that I might be complicit in such designs by not going out among the people more."

"Ma'am if I may," Charles hesitated.

"Go on. If you think there is something I should know, then tell me."

"Thank you, Ma'am. Some of the below-stairs staff came into contact with people handing out awful pamphlets in the market. They wisely brought it to the attention of Col. Biddulph, who then brought them to me. I will spare you their exact verbiage, but they made very disparaging remarks about Your Majesty, most of which are connected to your desire..." Charles looked for the least accusatory words, "...to not ingratiate yourself to the crowds."

"I see." Victoria found herself staring at the far corner again. "Everyone seems so interested in getting me out of this Palace. But I am comfortable here and see no reason to gadfly about just so people know I'm alive and well."

"Hyde Park is particularly lovely this time of year. Perhaps a short ride through to see the latest flower beds? That might appease your detractors a smidge."

"Oh, Charles, how Albert and I loved riding through the Park, especially this time in the late afternoon when the sun was low in the sky."

"Shall I send down to the Mews for a carriage to be brought around for you, Ma'am" Charles asked, perhaps a little too much hope in his voice.

"That won't be necessary," Victoria said flatly. "If the people want to see me so badly, they can wait a couple more weeks. I will be going to Windsor with Vicky then."

"Of course, Ma'am." Charles said, not disguising his disappointment one bit.

CHAPTER 4

Vicky's excitement for all things new did not slow down at the Channel. Louie and Billy were doing their best to keep their breakfast where they put it, but Vicky was all over the ferry to Ostend. She watched as the cliffs of Dover faded in the distance, and then peered across the water for the first signs of land like some great explorer from a bygone age.

Her excitement went into overload at her first sighting of a windmill as the train whisked them across the northern Belgian countryside. "They are absolutely beautiful, large and majestic. Yet, I can see how Don Quixote would have mistaken them for a monster!"

"They actually serve a very basic purpose," Billy informed the ladies as they were again traveling in an exclusive car, provided by Vicky's Uncle Leopold, the Belgian King. "Those large arms catch the wind, causing it to turn. This then causes a mill wheel to turn which grinds wheat into flour."

"My father has something similar on one of his estates, but it uses a local stream to move the wheel instead." Louise added.

"Fascinating," Vicky said absolutely mesmerized by the mechanics of how things worked. Her mother said she got it from her father. Focusing on the windmill gave her another occasion to wish her father had lived. If he was as half as interesting as everyone made him sound, he would have been a wonderful person to be around growing up.

The arrival into the capital of Brussels was less momentous to Vicky than the trip through unfamiliar lands had been. In many ways, it reminded her of London, causing her to wonder if cities everywhere were the same. Even the Belgian royal palace was remarkably similar to Buckingham. The big difference being the mood and the people.

There was a festive spirit in the palace as people were preparing for the next day's wedding. Vicky was met by her grand-uncle, King Leopold, a tall man who remained in remarkable shape despite his advanced years. Being now twice a widower, Uncle Leopold was joined in greeting his niece by his son and daughter-in-law, the Crown Prince and Princess. The younger Leopold was not as tall as his father, and was stouter, leaning in the direction of being fat. His wife, Marie Henriette, was a bit mysterious looking. She was from the Hungarian branch of the Habsburg family, and had jet-black hair topping her pale porcelain skin.

Uncle Leopold was a frequent visitor to Buckingham Palace, so Vicky was comfortable with him. But the rest of the day was spent being introduced to other far-flung cousins who she rarely, if ever, saw. The only Coburg relatives to visit England during her memory was her uncle Ernie Coburg and Aunt Feodora Hohenlohe. Now she was meeting Coburgs from eastern Europe and from Portugal, who all seemed so exotic compared to Vicky who was on her first trip outside of England.

And that was just her own relatives. There were also countless Archdukes and Archduchesses who were the groom's family. Vicky couldn't begin to keep them all straight. Max, the groom, was a younger brother of Emperor Franz Joseph. The Emperor stood out of course, because of his elevated rank. But it was his wife, Empress Elisabeth, known within the family as Sissy, who was the true star of that family. Her extraordinary beauty had all of the young men waiting on her hand and foot. The imperial pair were a young couple, with only two children so far, both daughters. As the children were still in the nursery, they were left in Vienna. Vicky understood that Austria followed Salic law which meant those little babies would never Empress. If Sissy had no sons, the Throne would go to Max, the man who was getting married the next day. So there was a still a chance that Cousin Charlotte might become an Empress.

***

The following morning, Her Royal Highness Princess Charlotte of Belgium, Saxe-Coburg and Gotha, Duchess of Saxony was a true vision of virginal beauty as she glided down the aisle of the royal chapel adjacent to the palace. Her hair was pulled back from her face so it's soft, china-doll-like features could be seen by all, even under the bridal veil.

Her groom, whose family were famed for their bushy beards sticking out in all directions, had trimmed his facial hair for the occasion, presenting a neatly groomed military officer whose blond hair presented contrast to his raven-haired bride. Not classically handsome, Maximilian was also not ugly, but simply plain, like so many of his bothers and cousins. The popular consensus of the day was the Habsburg men grew such outlandish whiskers to give their faces character otherwise missing.

As Vicky was representing her mother, she was afforded a place of honor in the seating of the guests, right next to the exiled Queen Marie Amélie of the French, the bride's maternal grandmother. As she had little in common with the elderly lady, she talked mostly with the guest to her left, the Duchess of Montpensier, who was representing her sister, Queen Isabel II of Spain. Vicky found her very interesting and rather exotic with her dark features. At one time the Duchess had also been, like Vicky, the heiress to a throne, but was displaced when the Queen, her elder sister, began to have babies.

As the Catholic service droned on in Latin, Vicky tried to be attentive, but found her mind drifting. She imagined what it would be like to be the bride. This led to her realizing she had not really ever known any boys or gotten the chance to have a crush because of her life sequestered away in the Palace. The closest she had come to male companions her own age were the children of her mother's cousin, the Duke of Cambridge. But even they were younger than she by just enough to be too childish for her to regard in any romantic thoughts.

She could not stop her mind from drifting to someone she only just met, the Duke of Saint Albans.

She imagined what a dashing figure he would be standing waiting for her at the altar of Westminster Abbey. Wait...what? She shook herself from her daydream just in time to follow the instruction to kneel and pray by the priest. *How can I even think such things? I only just met him. And he's a commoner despite his royal blood line.*

Vicky knew it would likely be her fate to be married to some princeling with little prospects, but who would have the family connections that would benefit the foreign office in some way. She sighed as the prayers ended and took her seat again until it was time to stand for the bridal couple's recession from the chapel.

During the luncheon that followed, Vicky found herself among a very different collection of neighbors, thanks to the standard boy-girl-boy-girl seating arrangement. To her left was her second cousin, the King of Hanover, a man nearly her mother's age and blind as a bat. However, he did not allow his loss of sight slow him down. He deftly managed his eating utensils and drinking glasses as if there was no impairment. However, his constant grousing to whomever would listen about the problems he had with his *diet*, the German equivalent to a parliament, became something of a bore to those around him. His other favorite topic of discussion was the aggressiveness of Prussia, Hanover's neighbor to the east. This line of conversation was something his other neighbors at dinner could share, much to the chagrin of Prince Friedrich of Prussia, who was seated directly across from Vicky.

The Prussian prince was the nephew of the current king, Friedrich Wilhelm IV. However, since the king was childless, Friedrich, known to all as Fritz, was the eventual heir to the throne, after his father. Fritz tried to appease his fellow German monarchs in attendance that Prussia was not planning to invade any of their countries and that he looked forward to a time when he would be discussing mutually-beneficial alliances with all of them. His entreaties fell on mostly deaf ears as everyone knew it might be a long time before this young man came to the throne.

However, Vicky hung on his every word and marveled at how different he was from everything she had always heard about the Prussians. She had been raised to view them as militaristic and a potential threat to her neighbors, whose territories the Prussia she thought she knew longed for. She also could not help, since the seating pattern forced her to be face-to-face with him across the table, to note how handsome he was. His strong muscular jawlines were shaved to show only a chinstrap of a beard. His hair was light brown and softened the ferocity of his emerald eyes.

As she tried to soak in the look and words of the Prussian prince, her thoughts were constantly interrupted by the antics of the guest to her right, the young prince representing the Russian Tsar. He had the misfortune of being seated next to a very young, maybe seven or eight, archduchess who was threatening to have a tantrum out of boredom in the stuffy formal dinner.

The prince was attempting to entertain her. He had been making funny faces and odd popping noises with his mouth. She soon tired of those antics, so he began softly drumming familiar tunes on the corner of the table using his silverware. Although he tried to be quiet, he soon gathered scornful looks from the great matrons around the table. It was clear their attitude was he should ignore the child, and if she fussed too much, she would be removed from the table and get no meal.

In his efforts to amuse the young Habsburg girl, he jostled in his seat rather often, occasionally bumping Vicky's arm. At first, she gave him annoyed looks until she realized why he was gyrating in his seat so. She watched with silent fascination his various attempts to keep the girl engaged. However, she could not contain her own laughter when the game course came and the prince, running out of ideas to be amusing, resorted to picking up his duck with his fork and guided the fowl in a spirited, if somewhat droopy, waltz around his plate. Vicky's laughing drew the attention of several others at the table, who either were very amused, or not amused at all.

Unfortunately, among the not amused was the young archduchess. In a final attempt, Nikolaus began humming a soft can-can to the girl complete with having the duck kick up its legs at the appropriate parts of the song. That was the final straw for the girl's mother, who was seated down and across the table a few seats. She signaled in the air and a nanny swooped in, plucked the child from the table, and was out a side door before the poor thing even realized she wasn't getting any dessert.

The other guests returned to meals as if nothing had happened. Vicky complimented her neighbor on his valiant efforts. "You must have younger siblings to go to such effort."

"Yes, I have three younger brothers who often have to be entertained during these grown-up affairs."

"I often wonder what it would like to have a bigger family like that. Sadly, I have no brothers or sisters," Vicky said.

"You are welcome to my two younger sisters. They tend to try my patience a bit."

"Oh my, there are six of you?"

"Seven actually, I have an elder sister too, but she got married just last year."

"I can't even imagine living a house with that many. We don't even have that many young people in the whole palace, even counting the children of the ladies-in-waiting," Vicky lamented.

"Oh forgive me, I am being most rude...I am Duke Nikolaus of Oldenburg." the young prince introduced himself. "Please call me Niko. It helps keep me and the other Nikolaus' in my family straight."

"And I am Vicky, daughter of Queen Victoria of the United Kingdom."

Vicky, now looking at him proper, and not over his shoulder at his antics with the girl, realized he was about her age, and rather handsome. She also noticed he was wearing a Russian military uniform, which she asked him about.

"Although my family is from a German Duchy, situated close to Denmark, I am from a younger branch which has lived in Russia since my grandfather married one of the sisters of the recently deceased Tsar. In fact, I am at this wedding as the representative of the current Tsar, who was unable to come himself."

"Very much like me," Vicky said. "My mother does not like to travel, so I am here representing her. The bride is her first cousin."

"How fortunate for me, otherwise I would not have such a beautiful companion to dine with."

Vicky blushed, not knowing how to respond. She had never been called beautiful by a boy before. Her mother often gushed on about how pretty she was, but she was her mother; that was her job. Coming from this perfect stranger, it meant something quite different. She liked the way it made her feel.

Niko continued, "I hope you will honor me with a dance at the ball this evening."

"I would be delighted." Vicky said smiling widely at him.

***

The ball that evening was the crowning event to culminate the wedding festivities. The ladies were in their finest gowns and jewelry, and gentlemen were typically in their dress military uniforms. While Louie accompanied Vicky into the ballroom, Billy Saint Albans was relegated to standing along the outer wall with all of the other foreign security personnel, though they all also wore their ceremonial uniforms to better blend with the surroundings.

He selected a spot close to a door that led form the ballroom onto a portico with steps to the gardens. He viewed this as the most unsecure entrance, although he took note that the entire grounds were being well policed by the King's private police force.

While his primary purpose for being there was to protect the Princess Royal, he amused himself by watching the royals dance and prance about the ballroom. Some, like the ever elegant King Leopold, glided effortlessly to the music, while others, notably the equally elder Prince from Holland, seemed to moving to a different beat only they could hear.

One odd thing he observed was from the Austrian imperial couple. If a gentleman wanted to dance with the empress, they did not ask her, they asked her husband. If he approved, then she was whisked away, regardless of her own thoughts on the subject. Of course, he could not help but to notice if the gentleman asking was young and dashing, he was denied permission. *Oh, the oddities of royalty*, he thought.

Princess Vicky didn't seem to have any of these weird quirks that he could tell. He was struck by how typical a girl she actually was. He was surprised when she talked about how few children were around her growing up. Perhaps it was her friendship with Louie that helped her find normalcy.

He watched Vicky as she took to the dance floor with that Oldenburg duke from Russia. She was quite the vision in a summery teal colored gown, her face surrounded by sapphires borrowed from the queen. The diamond and sapphire tiara she wore really stood out against her ebony hair. The matching earrings and necklace created a perfect frame for her face, causing her dark eyes to shine like onyx. While traveling, he didn't really have the opportunity to appreciate the hour-glass form of her body, something her gown illustrated beautifully.

The dancing continued well past midnight, with a promise that dawn might break before the music stopped. While Vicky danced with several different partners throughout the evening, Billy could not help but notice she seemed to return to the young duke frequently. At a little after one in the morning, he was guiding her to the doors to the portico where Billy had taken up his vigil. As they passed out into the night, Billy started to follow at a discreet distance behind, quickly joined by Louie. When Vicky noticed them, she told them both their presence was not needed. Billy began to protest on security grounds, but the princess assured him she would be safe enough being escorted by Duke Nikolaus.

They did as he was told, but Billy turned to Louie, "Yes, but who will guard her *from* Duke Nikolaus?" The response was nothing but a nervous giggle.

CHAPTER 5

"So Niko, tell me about Russia," Vicky was looking for something to talk about. "I envision this exotic far away land."

"There are parts that are rather exotic, but they are mostly in the southern regions. You must remember Russia is a gigantic country that covers nearly a fifth of the land on this planet. Therefore, we have a little of everything. But the places where most of the people live, either St. Petersburg or Moscow, are in the northern portion and get to be very cold."

"I am told that Scotland can get quite cold in the wintertime as well. I have not been there yet."

"How odd that you are the heiress to a rather small country and you have not visited much of it."

"We are *not* that small," Vicky pointed out with some pride, "especially when you consider all of our overseas territories. Canada alone is second in size only to Russia, plus we have the whole continent of Australia."

"Which is still an island," Niko observed.

"But a very large island," Vicky countered.

By this point they had walked some distance from the palace towards the rear of the grounds, discovering a small pond. Vicky used the occasion to sit on one of the benches near the pond to rest her feet.

"At least in Australia, I bet they swim, with all that water around them," Niko said.

"I imagine they might."

"It is a good thing that Russia got to keep the northern coast of the Black Sea after the war. It is about the only place we have warm enough to swim. Do you like to swim?"

"I have never been."

"What? you live on an island nation and can't swim? Well look here, we have a small pond. A perfect place to learn, not deep enough to drown in. And the air is very humid tonight, getting in the water would be very refreshing."

"I don't think my ball gown would find it very refreshing."

"Oh just take that off. God knows you ladies wear enough under things to be able to lose half of them and no one would know the difference." With this Niko started removing the outer portions of his uniform.

"What on Earth are you doing?" Vicky cried out.

"I thought that was obvious. I'm going to teach you to swim."

"What? You expect me to strip down, right here, in front of God and everyone?"

"I promise you, God has seen you naked, beyond that I *am* 'everyone'. Besides, you only need to go down to your bloomers, then when you get out you can throw the other fifty layers on and pull them off from underneath."

44

Vicky looked around wondering how often people walked this way. It was rather remote here, and it *was* two o'clock in the morning, as a chiming church tower in the distance told her. By this time Niko was naked from the waist up and busy fighting to get his boots off. His torso was quite attractive, slender but muscular, with just a hint of a trail of hair beginning in the center of his chest and traveling southward to...well to where she dared not think about. Yet, she found herself wanting to trace it with her fingers.

Now Niko was down to just his underwear, a rather snug fitting pair of cotton-looking shorts that she saw left little to the imagination when he turned towards her. "Well?" he asked. "If you want any of this," he indicated his body, "you'll just have to join me in the water." And he splashed to the middle of the pond where he still had to squat a bit to get under the water to his neck.

Alright, Vicky, she thought to herself, *you wanted to experience the world. This is definitely an experience you won't get in "Buck House."* She undid the numerous clasps and ties that held her gown in place and carefully removed her mother's jewels. Once her outermost gown was off she used it to protect and hide the jewels, just in case someone did come along.

"C'mon in, the water is wonderful tonight!" Niko called to her.

"Keep your voice down, do you want to get found?" Vicky chastised in a stage whisper.

Niko looked around, pretending to be very afraid and then ducked his head under the water. When he didn't come up right away, Vicky called to him as quietly as she could. "Niko?" He still did not surface. "Niko, this is not funny." But no Niko.

Having just removed her own shoes, she quickly shucked her petticoats and stockings. Being in nothing but her bloomers and camisole, she ran into the water to search for Niko. Just as she reached the last place she had seen him, he pushed up through the surface and grabbed Vicky in his arms. He fell back into the water, pulling her under the surface with him.

Vicky began struggling in his arms, hitting at him, and kicking with her feet. He quickly let go. Not immediately realizing she was free of him, she continued to kick and swing her arms, and soon found her head above the water. It took her only a moment to get her feet under her. As she felt the sandy bottom of the pond she quickly discovered she could stand up and the water only came up to just below her neck, just high enough to cover her breast. This was something she was quite grateful for when she discovered how see-through her camisole had become when wet.

"What was that?" she demanded, yelling louder than she intended to.

"Your first swimming lesson," Niko smiled broadly. When he stood all the way up, the water only came to the bottom of his chest. Vicky had never considered the idea of men having nipples before and found his rather fascinating.

"How was *that* a swimming lesson?" She tried to clear her thoughts, both from the dunking she just had, as well as the growing realization she was nearly naked in her great-uncle's pond...with a man!

"When I let go, you kicked your feet and paddled your arms...your technique will need to be worked on, but you were swimming."

"But you lied!" she chastised him. "About the water; it is freezing in here!"

"This is nothing. If you want freezing, try swimming in the Neva," Niko retorted. "Besides would you have gotten in if I said it was a little chilly?"

"Of course not."

"So, why tell you?"

With that she splashed him and he splashed back. Soon they were having a grand water battle.

"There they are! I knew I heard someone over here!" Niko and Vicky almost didn't hear the police officer cry out over the water play. "You there! Get out of there! That is the private property of His Majesty the King!"

"And I am a guest of His Majesty," Niko boldly proclaimed. "Nikolaus Petrovich, Duke of Oldenburg at your service, sir."

"Your Highness, please forgive me, without your uniform, I have of no way of telling you from some vagabond who has snuck into the palace grounds," the officer stammered.

"If the uniform helps, you will find it on the bench there," Niko responded.

The policeman took quick note of it and asked, "and I suppose you are the Queen of Sheba," he exclaimed eyeing Vicky as she was careful to remain submerged to her neck.

"The young lady is with me and that is all you need to know about her," Niko said quickly. Vicky was taken aback by his sudden show of gallantry and began seeing

47

him in an all new light. "I am quite happy to end our little swimming lesson as it now quite late I should like to retire for the night...er, morning rather. However, I must insist you turn your backs to us while the mademoiselle exits the water and gets dressed."

"With all due respect, Your Highness, standing there in your underwear, you are really not in a position to insist on anything. Now come on, the both of you out."

Vicky began to slowly move towards the pond's edge, the level of the water getting lower on her chest as she moved. She covered her breasts best she could with arms, but the clingy camisole might as well as not even been there.

"Louie!" came a cry from behind the police officer. Both Louise and Billy rushed to the bench where Vicky's clothes had been deposited. Vicky looked at them both dumbfounded while in mid-step, just shy of being indecently exposed. "How dare you run off, without my leave, with this...this...rag-a-muffin?" Louie scolded, doing her best to give Vicky a look to signal she should play along.

"And just who might you two be?" the policeman asked.

"I am the Princess Victoria of the United Kingdom, and this is Lt. the Duke of Saint Albans, from my personal protection detail," Louie responded affecting a haughty tone.

The police office bowed deeply to her. "My apologies Your Royal Highness, there are so many royal guests here, I'm afraid I do not recognize all of you on sight."

"Nor is there any reason why you would, officer," Louise responded in a kinder voice toward him. "If you please, this young lady is my lady-in-waiting. When she did not appear to attend me upon leaving the ball, I asked Lt. Saint Albans to accompany me while we searched for her. I had had the silly thought she might have fallen into some sort of trouble. I had no idea *this* was the sort of trouble, however."

"I see," said the police officer. After a little thought, he continued. "Well, as she is your servant, I will leave any discipling to you. But what about this Duke of where-ever-he-said, Ma'am?"

"I am quite sure it would be difficult for me to identify any man in such a state of undress." For emphasis, Louie opened the fan she had been carrying and used it to block Niko's nearly naked body from her view so she only saw his head. "But yes, I do know that face. He is the Duke Nikolaus of Oldenburg. He is here as a representative of the Russian Tsar. Perhaps the Russian ambassador could give better guidance in this matter."

"Thank you, Ma'am. In which case I will withdraw, with the young duke." Two other police officers each grabbed one of Niko's arms while a third gathered his clothing. They walked him off in the direction of the palace, despite his protests.

Once all of the other men were out of sight, Louie took Billy by the shoulders turning him until he faced away from Vicky, still mostly covered in the pond. Once his eyes were pointed in a safe direction, Louie signaled for Vicky to come ashore. Once there, she quickly helped Vicky back into dry clothes, gathering the wet ones from her as she went.

"Oh dear, what do you think will happen to Niko?" Vicky asked.

"Not bloody enough," Billy finally spoke up, anger clearly in his voice. "Marching him away like that was purely for your benefit, or rather Louie's actually."

"Yes Louie, that was quite clever of you impersonating me. A bit bold perhaps, but clever, nonetheless. However did you know to come here to save us?"

"I assure you there was no 'us' in our intentions. We waited thirty minutes and when you did not return, we became concerned."

"But I told you to remain in the ballroom. I was perfectly safe with Niko."

"Aye, we can see how 'safe' you were." Billy protested, his back still to the ladies.

"Besides, you did not tell us to remain in the ballroom," Louie pointed out. "You only said we need not accompany you. You didn't say anything about the two of us taking our own tour of the gardens. And as it turned out, it was for the best we did." Louie found it prudent to not mention they intentionally took their "own stroll" in the same direction they had seen Vicky and Niko go. "At least we got out of that without having to identify your maid by name. While protecting your reputation was paramount, I think I might still yet get to keep mine."

"You can turn around now, Billy," Vicky finally said once she had her evening gown and jewels mostly back in place.

"How could you be so reckless?" he exploded. "That randy Russian duke could have done God knows what to you once he got you in the water like that!"

"Calm down. It was nothing but some harmless flirtation."

"Harmless? If your mother found out about that, *you* would only be locked in a tower like Rapunzel. But *I'd* be serving the rest of my military career, if there even was one, in the jungles of deepest darkest Africa."

"Then you should also appreciate Louie's quick thinking. Thanks to her, Mama will never know." And with that simple explanation Vicky marched off towards the palace, leaving Billy and Louie no choice but to follow her. Being behind her they could not see the long breath Vicky let out, nor her blushing face as she dwelled on Duke Niko and how he looked while swimming or standing outside the water for that matter.

***

About noon the following day, the royal wedding guests were taking their leave and beginning their journeys back to their own lands. It had taken Vicky a long time to get to sleep after her adventure in the park. Once Billy had escorted her to her room and retired for what was left of the night, she was finally free to gossip with Louie. After finally giving up on the pursuit of a reason for men to have nipples, sleep came to her just as the sun was rising.

Now, in the palace's great entrance hall, Vicky found it difficult to force herself to stay awake and try not to think about her hungry belly as she had to skip breakfast in order to get out the door for the trip home.

While they waited for their carriage to come around to take them to the train station, Vicky looked at the other guests similarly waiting. She did not see the face she was looking for. The crown princess was graciously helping the king make the farewells. Vicky approached her.

"Has Duke Nikolaus already left?" she asked.

Henriette looked at her father-in-law, not quite sure how much she should say. The king came to her rescue.

"I'm afraid after last night's incident, it was deemed best for all concerned if he exited the palace immediately. I understand he went to the Russian Embassy."

"I'm sorry you were bothered with that little spectacle, Uncle," Vicky responded, using every ounce of concentration to keep her face as neutral as possible.

"How could I not? One of my guests behaving in such a manor, and out on the grounds where they were so easily discovered? I am only sorry you became involved. Your mother will not be amused to hear of this. Is your lady over there the young woman in question?"

Oh no! Vicky thought. *If he tells Mama about this, Louie will be removed from the palace. But if I confess to being the one in the pond, she might never let me out of the palace. And poor Billy, as he pointed out last night, serious harm could come to him and his career. Oh God! I have really messed this up.* While all of this went through her head, she stammered looking for an answer, glancing at Billy and Louie over her shoulder.

"Why Vicky, whatever is the matter?" Leopold asked.

Billy saw the look on Vicky's face, and stepped up to her.

"Your Majesty," Billy bowed to the king. "I think Her Royal Highness might be a little embarrassed by the whole affair. After all, as you might imagine, she likely has never encountered a man in such...a state," he left it there rather than saying something like "so nearly naked."

"Oh I see," smiled the king. "But Vicky, I'm afraid you will have to come to terms with that aspect of it your own, hopefully before having to discuss this situation with your Mama. I see no way of avoiding the topic as Lady Louisa is technically her lady-in-waiting."

Finally, Vicky hung her head in front of her great-uncle and confessed, almost inaudibly, "But Louie was not the one in the water."

Though an elder gentleman, King Leopold's physical prowess was in no way diminished, and this included his hearing.

"But why would you tell that to the police, then?"

Vicky was on the point of tears, looking for the words to admit what she had done. But it was Billy who rescued her once again.

"Sire, I believe the princess is embarrassed to talk of her own...kindness she showed in the heat of the incident. If I may?"

"What kindness? What the devil are you talking about, Saint Albans? Yes, continue," the king demanded.

"We don't know who the girl with the duke was, Sire," Billy lied, but did so with such conviction, Vicky could not help to wonder if maybe he had rehearsed this. "From her clothes we could only assume she was a lady from town whom the duke enticed into the pond with him somehow. The princess took pity on her and did not wish to see her humiliated, or worse, so claimed the girl was her maid, knowing the police would leave her alone. Once the police left, Vic..., er, the Princess Royal helped the girl to dry off and get dressed, then sent her back into town by whatever route she arrived."

"Vicky? I admire your mercy towards that poor girl, but you obviously did not think that through. Your Lady Louise's reputation and prospects would have been ruined had I reported what I was told to your mother."

"Then you have not written to her yet?" Vicky asked, maybe a little too hopefully.

The king sighed. He pulled a folded sheet of paper from inside his vest. It was sealed with the king's personal insignia. "I intended to give this to Saint Albans with the instructions to deliver it to none but the Queen. But now I see that I would have been presenting her with false information." He thought for a moment. "As the behavior of both you, and of the Lady Louisa, have been above reproach in this matter, according to what I have heard here today," he glanced at Billy. "I leave it to you whether you feel your mother might get a laugh from the events of last night. She will not hear of it from me." He ripped up the letter.

"Thank you, Uncle!" Vicky exclaimed with delight.

The king then turned to Billy, "And you sir; perhaps you took this assignment thinking your job was to only *physically* protect my great-niece? I see she is in good hands on all accounts." He winked at the young duke and, after kissing Vicky on the cheek in farewell, moved away to see off his other guests.

CHAPTER 6

"So tell me about this duke of yours," was the only bit of gossip from Brussels the Queen seemed to care about.

"Oh, Mother, now don't go thinking of him as *my* duke. After all, he lives in Russia so it is unlikely I will ever even see him again." They were sitting at breakfast on Vicky's first morning back at Buckingham Palace.

"But would you like to?" her mother asked.

"I'll admit he was very handsome. But he lacks responsibility and is even a bit rakish if truth be told."

"Yes, Aunt Fe told me there was some sort of incident with him involving a city girl and a pond?"

Vicky blushed crimson, busying herself with putting jam on a scone so she didn't have to look at her mother. "Where does that woman get her information? Well, I suppose when one's court is as small as Langenburg, they have to find amusements where they can."

"Careful Vicky, don't look down your nose at your Hohenlohe cousins. We might just have to go there to find you a husband."

"Mother, I am too young to be thinking about getting married. And besides, Charlie and Hermy are both a decade or more older than me and already have more forehead than hair."

"Hermann is only nine years older than you. We just might have to look for a little older for you. There are very few suitable bachelors among the royal houses that are your age. When I heard of this Niko of Oldenburg, I looked him up in the Gotha. He's only a year older than you."

"Stop matchmaking!" Vicky warned with feigned severity. She would never admit it to her mother, but she and Louie had spent many a rainy afternoon in the library going through the *Almanach de Gotha*, the who's who of European royalty, dreaming up romances or funny stories with this prince or that. She momentarily smiled to herself remembering the operatic tragedy they concocted for Princess Adelgunde of Bavaria, just based off of her name. But her mother was right. Husband material in her age range was far and few between.

"You're right. You are still a bit young. And that is too bad because I was going to ask if you wanted start helping me with my boxes," the Queen mentioned casually. "But if you're still too much a little girl —"

"I never said I was a little girl. I just said I'm not ready to discuss marriage yet," Vicky corrected quickly. The queen's boxes, which included all of the bills for her to sign and any other important documents from Parliament, was the very essence of the job of being queen. Vicky had been trying to get her mother to start sharing some of that part of her life with her for over a year, but had always be rebuffed with, "you're time will come." Was her time finally here?

"Very well, then. When we get back from Windsor, I'll start going through the boxes with you. But sweetheart, you really do need to start thinking about the future. You are my only heir, after all."

"Oh Mama, don't be silly. There are hundreds of people in a queue to succeed you. I just happen to be at the front of the line."

"But you're the only British one, so you might as well be the only one. I really don't think the British people would tolerate a foreigner King at this point. They barely accepted your father, no matter how hard he worked to win them over."

"But everyone always speaks so highly of Papa."

"People tend to appreciate what they lost only after they lost it," the queen sighed. Her vision clouded over and looked far into the distance as she always did when the late Prince Albert was mentioned. "You know you were almost supplanted in that first place in line. The doctors were fairly sure the baby I was carrying when your father was ... when he left us ... was a boy."

"Oh Mother," Vicky soothed softly, "we can't dwell on what might have been. For all we know, had Papa lived, you might have had eight or nine children. Just imagine the problem you would have had marrying all of them off."

"Bite your tongue, young one. As much as I love you, giving birth is the single worst experience my body has been through. And you would have me go through it a half dozen times or more, just to provide spouses to the courts of Europe? I think not. Your father, on the other hand, he would have liked a full nursery. But then, he'd have the easy part of creating all of those babies wouldn't he?"

Vicky giggled, and blushed slightly that her mother actually came close to mentioning sex. Deciding it best to change the subject before the queen got back to marriage, she asked, "So when are we leaving for Windsor?"

"I have to receive some new ambassadors on Tuesday, so I thought Wednesday afternoon would be a good time to travel."

"Oooh, I'll barely have time to unpack and then repack. I guess I know what I'll be doing after breakfast," Vicky said, dreading the task ahead of her.

***

The following week, John Stockley sat down at breakfast, unfolding the newspaper he had just gone out to get. While he was pleased to see the natives in India were in a full uprising against their Colonial occupiers, he scarcely scanned the headlines. He quickly turned to the page he bothered to spend the sixpence for to begin with, the Court Circular.

"So tomorrow's the big day, huh?" he said to the empty room. "O'course the heat o' the city's too oppressive for the high'n'mighty. I knew she'd be high-tailin' it to the countryside here pretty soon."

"Well, that's just fine. I'm almost ready." He walked over to a worktable covered with a tarp. Pulling off the tarp, he uncovered half a dozen nearly completed devices that looked like medium-sized sausages. But these "sausages" had notably metallic material inside their tubing and fairly short strings poking out of one end.

"All these need is a little wax coating, and they'll be good for pitchin'," he said as hefted one of them in his hand judging the weight, just as he had done while stuffing the metal shards mixed with gunpowder into the cow's intestines he had gotten from the butcher.

"She thinks it's hot here now. Jus' wait 'til one of these lands in her buggy."

***

"Well, Lt. Saint Albans, what do you have to say for your actions in Belgium?" Col. Everton-Smythe asked without preamble.

"Sir?" Billy asked, mostly to stall for time. He was not sure what his commander was referring to but was pretty sure he was about to find out. He had been racking his brain wondering how the colonel got of wind of the pond incident all the way from Brussels, but that was the only thing he could think of that warranted being called into the CO's office so unceremoniously. He only hoped he walked out with the same rank as when he walked in.

"Don't be modest, son. From the reports I have been getting, every female from the cutlery maids to not just a few princesses were wagging on about the handsome young man escorting the princess."

Billy blushed a deep red but didn't dare break his stance at attention. "I'm sure they were referring to the Duke of Oldenburg, sir," he finally answered when he could talk with a straight face.

"Oh yes, I heard about *him*, too." The Colonel dramatically rolled his eyes. "I supposed those Russian

59

boys' blood has to run a little hotter to make up for the climate."

At this, Billy was seriously in danger of laughing out loud. Everton-Smythe could see his discomfort and finally gave the command, "At ease, son." Billy relaxed his stance a bit and blew out a long breath to calm the giggle that threatened to escape his lips instead.

"Lieutenant, all reports of your behavior in Brussels have been impeccable. No doubt, it is due to your aristocratic background, but you have shown to be an excellent soldier to have in the room covering royal functions. This makes you a perfect candidate for the Royal Guard. While the Yeoman Guard protect the Queen and her family on a broader sense, patrolling the palace grounds, and standing watch at the doors, the Royal Guard protect the Family on a closer, more one-on-one, basis. I am assigning you to guard the Princess Royal anytime she is outside of the palace or during any larger events inside the palace. Your place is to always be no less than three and no more than five steps behind her. Is this understood."

Billy snapped back to attention. "Yes sir!"

"Son, keep your eyes open. The Home Office has alerted us that there are ill feelings growing towards the Queen among the populace. It is starting to feel like it did when her husband was murdered."

"I understand," Billy answered, even though he really didn't. How could anyone want to hurt the princess?

CHAPTER 7

Vicky was not sure how serious her mother had been about starting to show her the ropes of being a queen. Up until this point her mother had always shooed her away whenever she had official business to do or was meeting with her ministers. This is why she was pleasantly surprised when, at breakfast on the following Tuesday, the queen asked her to join her for the receiving of some new ambassadors.

As requested she arrived at the Throne Room thirty minutes early with Louise in tow, for instruction. She was met with a familiar face. "Billy? Why are you here?"

"I've been reassigned to the Royal Guard, and more specifically, to guarding you on a full-time basis."

"Well, I feel safer already, but whatever are you guarding me from in my own home?"

"I'm only here during public events, otherwise I will be with you anytime you leave the palace."

"Well, I'm sure my mother will be happy I have such attentive security."

"And what of you? Are you pleased?"

"To be honest, it disturbs me a little that I need to be protected from my own people."

"My superiors say there is some concern about a rise in anti-royal feelings. I'm afraid your mother's refusal to do more public events isn't helping her cause any."

"I try to get her out of the palace but moving a mule would be easier."

"Did I just hear you call me a mule?" Queen Victoria had turned the corner into the Throne Room at that moment. Billy snapped to attention and saluted.

"Oh my, Mama. The echoes in here distort things so terribly, wouldn't you say, Billy?"

Billy could do nothing but agree, hoping Vicky knew where she was going with this.

"I said you were going to teach me how to receive diplomats, and today's school would be easier."

"Easier than what?"

"Well, than his job of having to protect me."

"Mm-hmm," the queen was clearly not buying it, but decided to let it drop. "Well then, Saint Albans, you should take up your post."

"Yes, Ma'am!" He quickly took his position just inside the doorway to the Throne Room, happy to be out of that conversation. On the opposite side of the doorway was Captain Abel Smith, the queen's own personal guard.

Then the elder royal turned to her daughter, "and since when is Saint Albans 'Billy'?"

"He, Louie, and I became quite friendly during the trip to Brussels."

Her mother looked at her suspiciously. "How friendly?"

"You were the one to order him to never leave my side. I thought it only right to call him by his preferred name. And Louie was with us at all times," she added to try to appease her mother's worries.

"Oh never mind. If I dwell on this too much I'll have a headache and there too many diplomats to get through today."

Being her first time to witness this sort of event, Vicky was not sure what she would be doing. As it turned out, not anything at all. Her job was to stand still, look pretty, and smile at the new ambassadors as they approached. The queen did everything else. Vicky's real duty would be after they arrived, when she would attend a reception for them with her mother and have to make polite small talk as she circulated around the room.

As the first few arrived, it all went smoothly enough. By the time the third ambassador presented his credentials, it had all fallen into a routine. The Court Marshal called out the formal name and title of the ambassador, "His Excellency Count Gustaf Moltke, Ambassador from the Kingdom of Sweden", and then the person would walk in, usually with their spouse, bow low to the queen and present her with their official credentials from their own head of state assigning them as ambassador. There was a small table next to the queen, behind which stood her private secretary. She would hand him the folded documents and he would unfold and stack them neatly in a pile on the table. Meanwhile, the queen would engage for no more than thirty seconds in small talk, usually demonstrating some small trivia she knew of the ambassador's homeland.

Vicky was amazed at the all the details her mother was able to rattle off about even the most remote nations. She was also amused by the variations in what passed as formal wear in different parts of the world. One of the new ambassadors was from the tiny Kingdom of Tonga, situated in the South Pacific. Vicky was shocked and nearly embarrassed to the point of blushing as the man walked in wearing a knee-length skirt and a waist coast of bright and clashing colors, and nothing else. He had on no shirt, and nothing on his feet or legs below the knees. The open jacket displayed a torso devoid of any hair, the color of iced tea, and chiseled to the point that the movement of every muscle could be seen as he walked. It was all Vicky could do to keep her head from bobbing with his gait as he approached.

Still reeling from the sight, she was caught completely off guard by the marshal announcing the next and final ambassador of the day, "His Highness Duke Nikolaus, Ambassador from the Russian Empire." In marched Niko, looking absolutely resplendent in his red and blue uniform of the Imperial Hussars. As he was in uniform, he approached the queen, snapped to attention, and saluted instead of bowing. He handed her his credentials, "sent with the continued affection of my Tsar," he purred.

Victoria smiled widely. "I have fond recollections of His Imperial Majesty's visits to my country when he was Tsarevich," the queen responded. Raising one hand to her left, indicating Vicky, she continued, "and I believe you have already met my daughter, the Princess Royal."

"Ah yes, it was her beauty that inspired me to accept this assignment so far from my homeland."

Ignoring the over-the-top flattery, the queen responded, "I trust our warmer climate will appeal to you as well. Who knows, maybe you will consider making England your new home." She waved her hand to the right, indicating the interview was over, so Niko saluted again and withdrew to stand with the other ambassadors. The queen then made a few short welcoming remarks and invited them to enjoy refreshments.

Vicky had no sooner stepped off the dais to begin her rounds of circulating among the guests, when Niko was at her side. "Now that I am close at hand, perhaps we could continue those swimming lessons."

In a mild panic, Vicky looked around to make sure her mother had not heard. It would not have taken her long to put two and two together and come up with a pond in Brussels. Fortunately, the queen had gone to the other side of the room to start her mingling. However, she did turn and look at Vicky with concern right at that moment causing the princess to wonder if she heard even over the din of a crowded room. But, seeing her daughter chatting with Niko, Victoria just smiled and returned to her conversation with the Brazilian Ambassador and his wife.

"I believe we have had enough of those, thank you," Vicky finally responded coolly and moved to step away from the duke.

But he matched her step. "Then I look forward to the next activity I can teach you; perhaps rowing a boat down the Thames?"

"I'll take that under advisement." It was a phrase she heard her mother use often with politicians when she did not want to give an opinion, or better yet, to end a line of questioning. She then deftly raised her right hand to just over her shoulder indicating for her lady. Louie understood the nonverbal instruction and moved in between Vicky and Niko and began pumping him with questions about life in Russia, allowing Vicky to move on to a conversation with the next guest.

***

"So that was your young Niko?" the queen started after they had situated themselves in the carriage for the ride to the train station. She had been jumping from one topic to the next all morning as they prepared for their summer holiday in Windsor.

Vicky was used to this behavior from her mother anytime she was about to leave the palace. The thought of being out in public always agitated her and she could not focus on one conversation for more than a sentence or two. But now that they were seated and about to leave, Vicky hoped she would settle a bit, even if Niko was not the subject she would have picked to settle on. As a final touch, Lady Dorchester, one of the queen's ladies-in-waiting handed them each a beautiful bouquet of flowers to hold while they waved to their people.

"I've told you, he is not *my* Niko."

"No, but he clearly wants to be."

"He's an impetuous gadfly that doesn't know what he wants." Vicky found herself having to adjust her balance as the carriage pulled away from the interior court of Buckingham Palace. The parade, as she often called it, was under way. Ahead of the carriage were two members of the college of heralds acting as an honor guard carrying banners high up on long poles. The one the right carried the Union Jack while the one on the left, the queen's personal standard which quartered the historic arms of England, Scotland, and Ireland.

The queen faced forward in her carriage, with her daughter seated across from her. As this was not a state occasion, the carriage was a simple landau, with a roof that could be raised if the weather made it necessary. However, today was a beautiful sunny day with only a few fluffy clouds floating in the sky to keep it from getting too hot.

Next, the Duke of Saint Albans and Col. Abel Smith rode their horses directly behind the royal carriage, followed by a second carriage for the ladies-in-waiting. Bringing up the rear were six more members of the Royal Guard, riding side by side in three pairs.

"Well, Vicky, it seems he does know. After the reception yesterday, he returned to ask my permission to court you. He claimed he hopes to one day win your heart and your hand." Victoria gave her a daughter a knowing look, waiting for her reaction.

"What on Earth did you tell him?" By this time, they were about the leave the palace grounds and the first line of spectators were coming into view.

"Smile, dear. Wave like you were taught. Very good. I told him you were still too young to be courted seriously, but I was sure there would be opportunities for the two of you to see other in public settings. Would you like him to court you?"

Vicky just looked at her mother as if she had been asked the riddle of the Sphinx.

"I'll take that as a maybe," the queen smiled.

***

John Stockley stood leaning against the outside of the Royal Mews. He had been hanging around the area all morning so he could see which carriage was being used by the queen for her ride to the train station. He was pleased to note it was an open landau.

Though it was gearing up to be a warm day in late July, he kept his oversized coat on. No one would suspect he had a gunny sack with a handful of his "sausage grenades" in it hanging from his shoulder under the coat. He positioned the opening of the sack for easy access. He figured he would have time to light and lob only one, maybe two, of his makeshift bombs if he was fast enough. He weighed the option of throwing two at once, finally deciding that was the way to go. It wouldn't help to get one Victoria out of the way if another survived to carry on. But here he had a golden opportunity to get them both. By throwing two bombs, he could try to land them in both seats.

He saw the carriage as it turned out of the palace grounds and into the public street. It was still more than a hundred yards away though. He had to be patient. Wait for it to get close enough that he could not miss his target.

Fifty yards away. John took up his position a little closer to the road, standing next to a tree. He could lean his shoulder against the tree and look around it as he reached into his gunny sack. The bark was a perfect texture to light a match.

Thirty yards. He got one of the grenades out of the sack and reached for the second.

Twenty yards. He pulled a match from his coat pocket with his free hand and positioned it against the tree waiting to strike. He would have to do this in one fluid motion: strike the match, bringing it to the wicks, which he now held together so both could be lit at once, then spin around in the same direction to help propel the bombs into the royal carriage.

Ten yards, time to strike!

He pulled the match along the bark keeping his focus on the carriage... "what the Hell?"

***

Vicky wasn't sure how she felt about the idea of being formally courted by Niko, or anyone else for that matter. Trying not to dwell on the question, she began to look at the crowds that came out to see their queen. She had been waving to the people on her left, but as they approached the Royal Mews, the number dwindled a bit due to less room there for them to stand. She turned towards the larger crowd on her right just in time to see a man jump on the running board of their carriage.

Vicky reached out without thinking, not even registering the pistol in his hand. Nor did she notice the hand she stretched out had the bouquet of flowers in it until her arm was almost all the way extended. In a split-second decision, she bent her arm and swung it fiercely at the unwanted rider. The flowers caught his extended hand just under the pistol, forcing it upward. When it fired, she heard her mother scream, along with several people standing along the road close enough to see what was happening.

The man was taken totally by surprise and started slipping off of the running board. Then many things happened at the same time. The carriage driver snapped his reins, forcing the horses to take off at a run. The gunman hooked his left arm over the side of the carriage, attempting to swing the pistol around for another shot, this one aimed at Vicky. Then a black wooden baton came from over the queen's head, connecting with the gunman directly in the face.

This time, the force of the blow made him release the pistol, which clattered into the floorboards. It also forced him off of the side of the carriage. As they sped away to safety, Vicky looked over her mother's shoulder to see Billy viciously beating the gunman with his baton as the remaining Royal Guards split into two groups, one helping Billy and the other approached to continue escorting the royal carriage.

She only vaguely acknowledged Col. Abel Smith now riding at full gallop next to the carriage, as she leaned forward to her mother. "Are you hurt, Mama?" she cried out.

Queen Victoria just sat there for a second her hand to her heart, as she breathed deeply, and in quick, short breaths. Finally, "I don't think so. Are you?"

"I broke my bouquet," was all Vicky could say. The queen just looked at her with the queerest expression and then started giggling. Vicky started giggling too at her mother's response. Soon they were laughing uncontrollably as the initial shock wore off them both, and the adrenaline drained from their bodies.

Then Victoria's face grew very serious and she grabbed her daughter into a full bear hug and starting sobbing. "Dankt Gott! Nicht ihr auch!" (Thank God! Not you too!)

***

John Stockley could do nothing but watch as the royal carriage sped away, moving too fast for him to be able to hit. Nothing but watch and suck on the burn on his thumb from the match he ended up not using.

CHAPTER 8
November 1858

"Not a single 'Regrets!'" the queen declared triumphantly.

"Congratulations, Ma'am," Grey responded in his usual flat, non-comital tone.

"Vicky will have all of Europe to choose from." Victoria beamed.

"And should she choose 'none of the above'"?

"That will not be an option. I have made it absolutely clear she must choose a future husband by the time she turns eighteen. The very fate of the kingdom hinges on this point. She's a conscientious girl, she will do her duty."

"As you command, Your Majesty." Grey replied, unsure who the queen was trying to convince, him or herself.

***

"But, what if I don't like any of them?" Vicky fretted to Louie. As her eighteenth birthday loomed ever closer, she faced it with growing dread. Ever since that scary day last year when that lunatic fired a gun at her and her mother, the latter talked of nothing but securing the succession for the future.

The would-be assassin, a man named Peyton, had turned out to be quite mad. He told the police that he not meant to hurt either lady but was aiming for some sort of demon he imagined was in the carriage with them. He was determined not fit to stand trial and would be spending the rest of his days in an asylum for the insane.

Meanwhile, Queen Victoria, retreated even farther from her people. She initially refused to even return to London at the end of her summer holiday. She was so dead-set against it, she even refused to receive her ministers unless they promised to not raise the issue. In the end, she relented, but only after constant harassment from Vicky, and finally the use of a secret weapon, Uncle Leopold. He was the only father figure the queen had ever known. He was able to talk sense into her, both as a mentor and her equal.

But even though she agreed to return, she would only do so secretly. No one outside the queen's immediate circle of servants who had to do the actual packing, Vicky, Louie, and their personal bodyguards were informed of the date and time they would travel. Even then, they arranged to arrive in London after dark and were driven back to the palace in a plain, unmarked carriage that was completely enclosed and with curtains drawn on the widows, to hide the royal occupants.

The Queen resumed her duties but any talk of leaving the Palace was strictly forbidden. Vicky was also kept a virtual prisoner. The only fresh air she got

74

was walking in the private grounds of Buckingham Palace, and then only with now Capt. Saint Albans at her heels. He was promoted after so valiantly pummeling the would-be assassin last year.

It was during these walks that she learned a great deal about her bodyguard. He had a younger sister, Diana, and his father had died when he was only nine. This explained why he was already a Duke at such a young age, which she found was one-and-a-half years older than herself. It turned out he did not care much for his step-father, Viscount Falkland, whom he nicknamed Faulty. Beyond these family dynamics, his life was all about his job protecting Vicky.

"Well, you're coming down to wire," Louie answered, bringing Vicky back to the present. "Perhaps it would help if you eliminated the non-starters before we even get to the ball."

"Well that is easy enough. We can probably rule out all the Catholics. It is unlikely any of them would be willing to convert."

"Okay, so no Habsburgs, Savoys, Liechtensteins or the three Bs —" Louise started checking off the list of invitees.

"The three Bs?" Vicky asked.

"Bavarians, Bourbons, and Braganzas. And they intermarry so much they are essentially one family anyway."

"Sadly, that also takes out Cousin Philippe. He seemed rather nice, even if a bit stuffy at his sister's wedding in Brussels. I also got the sense he does not want to leave Belgium, even though Uncle Leopold is trying to find a grand alliance for him. He is a Coburg, so maybe he would be willing to convert, and he is a second son, so not expected to inherit his own throne. Of course that would be a little more certain if his brother would have a son, but so far only one daughter. Let's keep him in the maybe column."

"Check." Louie made dramatic gesture of moving her hands from her right to directly in front of her as if she was actually moving his name. Vicky smiled at her and was starting to get into the game.

"I guess we also need to take out of consideration any Crown Princes. I'm pretty sure the government would never allow us to join with another country. This is really too bad. I was very impressed the Fritz of Prussia. His ideas for his county are so far removed from the militaristic leadership they have had thus far. If I wasn't going to be Queen here, I could easily see myself being his instead."

"Maybe he has a brother? You could build a connection that way," Louie suggested.

Vicky picked up the copy of the *Almanach de Gotha* that had been on a permanent loan to her while she got ready for this ball. She was expected to know all the foreign guests inside and out before they arrived so she could make an informed decision. She called it shopping for a husband from a catalog.

"Nope. An only sister. It looks like the only other eligible bachelor is a distant cousin named Albrecht." She looked at Louie expectantly.

Louis went to the desk and searched thru a list she picked up. "Yes, here he is. Prince Albrecht of Prussia, age 21. So yes, he has already been invited."

"Of course he has. Mama would not have missed a bachelor so close in age." Vicky rolled her eyes. "Okay, he's on the 'real possibility' list, I guess. Although I know absolutely nothing about him."

Louie was looking the list up and down, as she had so often before. It was her job to also learn who all these eligible princes were so she could help Vicky in case her memory momentarily failed her. "Well that gets us down to one Hessian, one Baden–who is reported to be a bit off–and then some from the minor duchies and principalities. Oh wait, I forgot Denmark. The new Crown Prince, Christian of Glücksburg, he has a couple of sons." She followed her finger down the list. "Never mind, one is destined to be King and the other is only thirteen."

"Slim pickings." Victoria said. An assessment she had held of her royal choices for quite some time now. Yet, she kept hoping to find someone she overlooked.

"Well, there is the one obvious choice..." Louie started.

"Don't even say his name!" Vicky ordered.

"You know you are going to have to consider him at some point."

"He is completely unacceptable. He is unreliable, unsophisticated, ..."

"From a reigning family, has close ties the Tsar, is already based in England... and so handsome!" Louie interjected.

"Yes, he is *all* of that too," Vicky conceded. "Damn it, Niko! Why can't you have some substance between your ears?"

"Vicky! Language!" Louie mock-scolded.

"You see why he is so unacceptable. He brings out the worst in me!" Vicky giggled.

"But he does get you to speak from the heart. Otherwise, you would not be so passionate in your denials." Louie beamed.

Vicky momentarily considered throwing the *Almanach* at her.

***

"Gentleman, gentlemen, this is madness!" the Prime Minister exclaimed. Edward Smith-Stanley, 14th Earl of Derby had taken over the premiership from Palmerston only nine months ago and was already sorry he did so. Between mending broken alliances over the botched assassination of Emperor Napoleon III, which is what brought down the prior government, and the ongoing efforts to wrest control of East India Company from it proprietors to be placed under direct control of the Crown, he did not have time to stir up a hornet's nest with the Queen.

But that was what Lord John Russell was proposing. A radical MP from London, he was constantly on the reform path. Whether it was the treatment of Catholics at home, or affairs abroad, he was always seeking to shake up the establishment and reform it under his own guidelines. So it should have been no surprise to anyone, he now wanted to take on the monarchy itself.

"If this country is to remain a monarchy, it must have a participating monarch!" Russell roared over the din of loud murmuring on the Commons floor. For emphasis he pounded the table where his bill was lying for first reading. It proposed establishing a Regency, in light of the fact that the Queen had all but abandoned her position, and named the Princess Royal to be the Regent, effective on her eighteenth birthday in a few weeks, or the passage of the bill, whichever came first.

"But this proposal is tip-toeing dangerously close to treason, sir!" Derby yelled back.

"It is not treason for the government to govern, and in doing so, it is perfectly legitimate for us to demand of our hereditary head of state to perform her duties. If she does not, then she should pass the authority of the Crown to someone who will." This set off a shouting match in which no less than twenty members were all yelling at one time and no one was able to listen adequately to any of it.

"Order! Order!" Mr. Speaker yelled over and over, until the House settled a bit. "Surely the Honorable Member must concede the Princess Royal is still a child. Not only would you be asking her to take up the job of reigning in her mother's stead, but most likely in direct opposition of Her Majesty."

"Mr. Speaker, you have heard the crowds in the street. If we don't so something to appease them, we might just loose the monarchy altogether. They're calling for a republic and the sentiment is quickly going the way of the French just sixty years ago. During which time, I would remind you, they have already gone through two republics interspersed with the Napoleonic Empire, a restoration of the Kingdom, and are now on their second stab at the Bonapartes." Another round of yelling ensued. Lord Derby rose for attention. Once the Speaker had settled the House again he acknowledged him. "Mr. Prime Minister?"

"Mr. Speaker, in essence, I am not entirely sure this such a crazy idea." Loud murmuring started again.

Derby waited. "However, this proposal has come before us without preamble or warning. It is a very ..." he looked for the right word, "...novel approach to the situation with Her Majesty. It is my humble opinion that she is truly not aware of the direness of the situation that her reluctance to leave the palace has placed her and us. I would therefore recommend a delegation of two Members and two Lords be appointed to advise Her Majesty of this course of action we might have to consider should she continue. Hopefully, we can get her to see the need to be a little more active in her role. Furthermore, I would recommend this delegation be made up of those she would consider friendly faces, and people with *successful* track records in negotiation." He stressed the word successful while staring directly at Lord John, clearly indicating he be excluded from such a delegation.

"This a wise suggestion. Will the honorable member withdraw his bill for the time being pending proper notification to the Sovereign?"

"I will not!" Lord John exclaimed. "That woman has thwarted her duties for near two decades now. A few days more will make no difference."

"Very well, seeing no second, the Bill is denied on first reading." The speaker quickly hammered his gavel before anyone could say otherwise. "Next order of business." Pandemonium exploded with cries of "second", "point of order", and "jolly good job" mixed in the cacophony.

As Derby left the floor, Lord Palmerston, who watched from the galley, caught up to him. "Now

Teddy, the hard part. You have to find four faces the Queen would consider friends."

***

Selecting four people to walk boldly into the lion's den was even harder than Derby expected. Having only served as Prime Minister a few months, he had yet to face the Queen's full fury. Nonetheless, he was happy with his delegation: Benjamin Disraeli, leader of the loyal opposition, who the Queen had always regarded warmly; Lord Edward FitzAlan-Howard, younger son of the Duke of Norfolk, though a commoner himself, was born at the pinnacle of the nobility and could address Her Majesty on near equal terms; the Duke of Sutherland, whose wife was Victoria's closest friend; and the ace up his sleeve, the Duchess of Buccleuch, one of Victoria's oldest friends and her former Mistress of the Robes. Derby decided to join them to help steer the conversation.

When the appointment to be received by the Queen was arranged, it was only for a delegation from the Parliament. She was not informed who comprised the delegation. The five arrived together at the appointed hour and were escorted to her majesty's receiving room. This spartanly decorated room was empty save a low dais upon which sat a throne-like over-stuffed chair, with decorative red velvet curtains hanging as a backdrop behind the Queen.

Upon seeing the lot in front of her, Victoria, called out her P.M. "Lord Derby, seeing the faces that have joined you today, I feel that I am about to be asked for something that I don't want to give." Then directing her attention to the Duchess, "Lottie, has Walter finally seen reason and ceded his seat in the Lords to you?" referring to her husband the Duke, who never made a parliamentary move without advice from his wife.

"Not quite yet, Your Majesty."

"Your Majesty," Derby started. "A bill came before the Commons recently that has raised great alarm among those most loyal to the monarchy, and to you personally. It called for a Regency to be declared and the Princess Royal to be named Regent." The look of shock on the queen's face was precisely the reaction he sought. He then quickly added, "be assured we have managed to suppress the bill...for now."

Disraeli spoke up next. "Your Majesty, there are growing demands from the populace that we take action. There have been demonstrations in every large city across the kingdom. The people want their queen. They feel abandoned by you. I think the final straw was last spring when you sent His Royal Highness the Duke of Cambridge to open Parliament on our behalf. It was the first time in living memory the Sovereign had refused to do this his or herself."

"Mr. Disraeli, We always find your knowledge of the law to be admirable." her use of the imperial We put him on guard. "Pray tell me, sir, where is it written the Sovereign must present their self to the people for physical inspection? It would seem to me, the only ceremonies We must attend are Our coronation, which We have already done, and Our funeral, which somehow I doubt anyone would let me miss." The queen's temper was starting to rise. "Our duties, such as they are, are to sign your bills into laws, and receive dignitaries as needed. If there are decisions to be made,

We can make them from here far easier than We could bouncing around town in a carriage."

"And what of Your Majesty's brave soldiers?" the Duke of Sutherland asked. Of those present, he was the only one to experience the horrors of war firsthand, having been assigned to Prussian headquarters during the Napoleonic wars.

"What about them?" the Queen asked shortly.

"When they returned battered, bruised, but victorious from the Crimea, it was expected they would be welcomed by their Queen. But they were not. That duty fell, by default, to a variety of government officials. They fought for Queen and county, Your Majesty, not for the Minster of War and country. You also have not participated in any of the traditional military pageantry, not even the Trooping the Colour which also celebrates your own birthday. Ma'am, this extreme isolation must come to an end."

"Who are you to tell Us what We must do?!" the Queen yelled at the Duke.

"Ma'am," the Duchess of Buccleuch said quite softly, as if she was soothing an upset child.

"Et tu, Lottie?" the queen looked at her oldest friend with astonishment.

"Ma'am," she began again, with a stronger voice. "I, more than most, know your pain. I was there that horrible day in '42." She indicated the Duke next to her. "George, his Hattie, and I saw to you through that horrible time, the funeral, getting back into a carriage again. Yes, we know your pain, we lived it with you day-by-day. But a time comes when you must put the past where it belongs—behind you. Else, you may never move forward."

Lord Edward added the turning screw. "I'm afraid, Your Majesty, the country is moving forward and insists on doing so with, or without you. Moving forward without their queen might well be a fatal blow to the monarchy itself."

The Queen looked down. Tears were starting to form at the remembrance of those darkest first days without Albert. Then she thought of that madman who tried to shoot Vicky. Her resolve returned. She stood, at which everyone bowed or curtsied.

Through bitter tears she hissed, "if the people are so adamant We be in their presence then they should refrain from trying to murder Us!" and she stormed from the audience room.

"That went well," Lord Edward said, rolling his eyes after she left.

"Don't be so quick to declare defeat," said the Duchess. "We made our case. She has to come to her own conclusion. And there is still one person who might just get through to her."

***

Vicky found her mother where she expected to, in her father's rooms. News of what happened in the audience room spread quickly through the ladies' maids and Louie brought it to Vicky's attention as soon as she heard of it. Vicky immediately took charge of the situation, gave Louie her orders, then let the whole thing set for an hour. She gave her mother time to catch her breath, and cool her anger, before setting off to find her.

By the Queen's orders, Prince Albert's rooms were kept up as he would be returning to them at any moment. The linens were changed and laundered regularly. When the queen was at lowest spirits, this was her retreat. Here is where she felt closest to her dead husband, and here is where she would come to find guidance when she had problems.

"Oh Mama!" Vicky exclaimed when she saw her mother sitting on the bed, holding the shirt that had been laid out but would never be worn again.

"Leave me," Victoria ordered chocking back her tears. "I'll come find you later and we'll talk then."

Vicky knew from the sound of her mother's voice, it was her final word and it would only upset her more to try to force her to talk to her. So she left knowing this conversation was going to be beyond her. But the one person who might be able to help was just walking into the Palace.

"How do I do this?" Victoria asked into Albert's shirt. "How do I face the world out there without you? How do I keep Vicky safe?" she cried into the shirt, throwing herself onto bed, sprawled across Albert's clothes. After several minutes, she nearly screamed at the empty suit beneath her, "How do I go on?!"

"By shtanding up and toing it," came a firm, very German, voice in response.

Standing in the doorway was the last person Victoria wanted to see right now, yet it the one person she needed more than ever—her mother.

Princess Viktoria, the Duchess of Kent had always had a difficult relationship with her daughter. She spent Victoria's youth isolating the heiress, especially from what she considered the girl's degenerate

Hanoverian relatives. She tried to instill the values of her own Saxe-Coburg family, even to the point of conspiring with her brother, King Leopold, to help Victoria fall in love with their mutual nephew, Prince Albert. As it turned out, Victoria surprised them both and did that all on her own.

After the death of baby Victoria's father, Viktoria made the mistake that took her years to recover from. She placed her faith in the wrong man. Her comptroller, John Conroy, was a power-hungry snake who blinded the widowed duchess with flattery and talk of preserving her proper place within the royal family. His ultimate goal was to be co-Regent over Queen Victoria, assuming she would come to the Throne as a minor. He was only thwarted by King William IV's determination to live until Victoria turned eighteen. A feat he managed with great difficulty, and only by four weeks.

Upon becoming Queen, one of Victoria's first acts was to dismiss Conroy and order her mother to remain in Kensington Palace while she moved to Buckingham. This estrangement remained until she was due to give birth to Vicky. It was only then that Albert was able to orchestrate a thaw in relations between his wife and his aunt/mother-in-law.

Now the Queen was on friendly terms with her mother, even if she did keep her at arm's length. She saw no reason to change the arrangement of having them separated by Hyde Park. When they named their baby Victoria, Albert had joked, "no house can withstand more than two Victorias in residence at a time."

Wallowing in all of these memories, the younger Victoria threw herself into her mother's arms. Though she was 72-years-old, the Duchess was of sturdy German stock and could easily support her diminutive daughter's weight. "But I'm afraid," the younger woman admitted.

"I know you are, Trina." The Duchess, who only learned English after her marriage to Prince Edward, retained her strong German accent. Trina was a nickname derived from her daughter's full name Alexandrina Victoria. Though she was actually calling her baby girl Drina, her accent made it sound like Trina. The nickname stuck.

"Now they want to replace me!" the Queen wailed.

"Oh Liebchen. Tey don't vant to. But you haff given tem little choice. But my little birties in Parliament tell me tey have only fired a first shot to get your attention. It seems to me tey got it."

"But what should I do."

"First ting, dry your eyes. Ten, you vill be able to see again. Die answer is really very simple. Resume your public duties."

"But, what if they keep trying to kill me, or worse, Vicky?"

"Vat if, vat if...vat if a tree falls and bops you on your het? You can't control what utters do, only vat you do. You haff all tose handsome men protecting you, trust tem to do teir yobs."

Victoria smiled at her mother's reference to the handsome men.

"Now kommen, Liebchen. Let's leaf all tese unhappy memories, und see vat is on die calendar for tomorrow."

"But Mama, my memories of Albert are not unhappy. I keep this room this way to remind me how happy we once were."

"I know. And it vill still be here ven you need it again."

CHAPTER 9

The day after the "intervention," as she came to call it, Queen Victoria was happy to privately meet with her oldest and dearest friend, the Duchess of Buccleuch.

"Lottie, it is good to see you again," Victoria said as she hugged the Duchess.

"I am so sorry it was under such circumstances yesterday."

"The government made their point. I will make my own decision in due course." The Queen said, making it clear that subject was now closed.

"Well, I brought something of a peace offering to make up for my role in all of that," Charlotte said.

"But you don't need to, and you have no package with you."

"It's a little more complex than that and requires a little explanation."

"Go on," Victoria encouraged, a little amused. She did so love getting presents.

"I recently purchased a small estate not terribly far from Edinburgh. It is to be my refuge from the constant hustle and bustle of Dalkeith. The boys are all grown now, Junior just got married and he and Anna are living there until they set up their own house, and the older girls are away at school. I only have Mary with me now, and Dalkeith is just getting to be too much. It hasn't been announced yet, but Wills is getting married next year, and Walter and I are easing him into running the estate. Walter stays in London most of the year, and that left me needing my own space."

"I have always marveled at how you managed to raise all those children. And you have kept a decent figure on top of it. I thought I would never lose the weight I gained with Vicky. I hate to think what I would have looked like if we had the big family Dear Albert had wanted. And at my height, if I kept gaining, I would look more like a toad on a mushroom than a queen on a throne."

"Oh, I had a full staff of nannies and governesses to help, that's for sure. Anyway, this small castle I purchased, called Balmoral, came with more staff than I will ever need there. Apparently the family who owned it previously was feuding with another family and needed the extra security. I do not."

"I must say, you Scots seem to feud a lot," the Queen observed.

"We in the Scott family have always been fortunate to have large enough families to settle our disputes with marriage rather than mayhem."

"In my family they were often the same thing." Both ladies had a good giggle over that one. Victoria felt so much better having someone to just be "one of the girls" with. Maybe it was because Lottie had been her first Mistress of the Robes, and thus her first person to be close to after becoming Queen, or maybe it was because Lottie was nearly royalty herself, being the wife of a direct male-line descendant of Charles II's eldest, albeit illegitimate, son, but Victoria was always at ease in her presence. Lottie was to her what Louie was to Vicky.

"Back to my story," Charlotte continued. "There were several what the Scots call ghillies working at Balmoral. Technically they were groundskeepers and other outdoor staff, but in actuality, they were highly trained protectors of the estate from the family on the other side of the feud. One such ghillie was trained to also personally serve the masters of the house, being something between an equerry and personal bodyguard. If it pleases Your Majesty, he has agreed to enter royal service and serve as one of your personal bodyguards. I hope his presence will make you feel a less edgy about going out in public."

"This is all very thoughtful of you, Lottie, but won't he miss his family in Scotland?" the Queen asked.

"He is unmarried. He has several siblings, and they are now spread all over the kingdom, many of them in service to other prominent families. In fact, one of his sisters is a maid in Marlborough House."

"If she can handle working for Uncle Sussex, she must be made of stern stuff." Victoria rolled her eyes.

"I assure you, that does run in their family."

"So when can I meet this ghillie?"

"Right now if you wish." Charlotte rose and went out into the hall. She shortly returned with a tall, muscular, not unattractive man in a kilt. "Your Majesty, I present Mr. John Brown."

***

With a little more encouragement from both Viktoria her mother and Vicky her daughter, Queen Victoria finally made a public appearance. While it was Capt. Abel Smith who oversaw all the security arrangements and rode on one side of the queen's carriage, it was Mr. Brown who rode on the other side, and accompanied the Queen after she departed the carriage.

She made a point to make her first outing to a hospital caring for the long-term rehabilitation of soldiers from the Crimean War. She also made sure to address the crowd that awaited her when she arrived, some of whom were protesting the monarchy.

From the stairs leading into the sanitarium, the Queen made her remarks. After a few brief canned comments about being proud of the British Forces who fought in Crimea, she faced the small contingent of protestors who were kept off to one side and behind the friendlier faces., almost out of her sight. Almost, but not quite.

"You there," she called loudly, "Yes, you, holding those placards. If put down the signs, I'll ask the policemen to allow you to come closer." She was actually yelling to be heard by them. They looked at each other, confused what to do. Most of them did as they were asked and handed their signs to others who seemed not so inclined to trust the police. Once they were free of signs or any other potential weaponry, the police allowed them to mingle in the crowd just in front of the queen.

"Now, that is better. I don't have to yell so loud, and I really want you to hear this. I am well aware that many of you have been disappointed that I have not been out in public as much as you might like." She paused as the newcomers murmured their agreement with this. The more polite society who had previously been staged at the base of the steps, just looked on, not sure how to react to the Queen going off script.

"Well, despite what some of the seedier press has said, I assure you I have not been shirking my responsibilities, nor have I gone mad, despite having a teenaged daughter." That got a few actual laughs. "I have been signing bills, meeting my ministers, and the rest of that tiresome prattle you never see." This got a few smirks from the crowd. "But I have been doing something even more important. I have been ensuring the continuation of our very kingdom. The only way for me to be do that was to raise my daughter to be able to continue after me. While she was still a child, I had to keep her protected.

"My grandfather might have had his problems." This unexpected admission brought several snickers from the audience who was hanging on her every word. "But in some ways, he was very lucky. He had fifteen children, his wife, and a few brothers to assist him with all things he had to do as King. Since the death of my beloved husband, I have had me, just me, with a little help now and then from my cousins. Well, between you, me, and this post," she knocked on a pillar that was on the side of the staircase, "I am looking very forward to my daughter's birthday in a few days when she will be an adult and can do a little of it in my place. And let's all keep our fingers crossed she finds her Prince Charming like I did, who can be even more helpful." The Queen then did something so un-queenly the crowd broke out into instant applause. She winked at them.

What the crowd did not see was the very deep breath she took and let out once she was inside, nor did they see how badly her hands were shaking. John Brown did though.

Once she got the first appearance out of the way, a few others followed, and flowed much more according to plan. Though she was terrified each and every time her carriage left the gates of the Palace, she learned to swallow her fear and put on a good show. John Brown became a godsend, and his presence always managed to calm her.

He had a way of knowing just the right thing to say or do to reassure her. He spoke in a thick Scottish brogue, which Victoria found delightful, and always broke things down to the least complicated statement that he could. His directness was a respite from all of the puffery the more experienced royal staff used.

***

John Stockley just leaned against the tree he had stood under during the Queen's arrival.

All this drivel about raising her daughter. What a load of crap. She had more servants than she even knew about to do that for her. No, he had seen her face after that nutter outside Buck House fucked up his plans last year. She was scared to leave the palace, pure and simple.

I wonder what changed. Why is she out and about now? Betcha the politickers had a come to Jesus meeting with her! Good, that means we are getting to them.

And she seems to have a new bodyguard now, a Scot. He's a big bloke. Might have to find a way around him...or a way to remove him.

***

While the Queen was feeling her new legs outside of her cocoon, the Palace staff, and Vicky and Louie in particular, oversaw every little detail of the pending birthday ball. It was Vicky who assigned quarters to the foreign guests. She ranked everyone by closeness of relation, and of importance with foreign affairs, and assigned accommodations accordingly. So while her close Hanover and Coburg cousins got to stay in Buckingham Palace, the Romanoffs, still smarting from recently being kicked out of Crimea, were placed at a safer distance, in St. James' Palace.

She also put the Catholic guests all together in Kensington. Not only did it have the room to accommodate them all, but it also was very close to Brompton Oratory should any of them have a desire to attend mass.

"But you have not provided a room for Duke Nicholas," Queen Victoria noticed when looking over her daughter's plans. Of course, Victoria had fixated on the young Russian duke, considering him the best possible match for Vicky.

"He already lives in London, Mama, and does not need to stay in one of the palaces. It was you who invited *all* of Europe, and we need to be a little economical with the space."

"How very practical of you. I had to invite *everyone* so all of these eligible bachelors I am lining up for you will have other princesses to dance with as well. I daresay, I doubt your father could have managed this any better. You have grown to be so like him. I do wish he would have been here all these years to help guide you."

"Besides," Vicky continued before the queen became too melancholy, "I am quite happy to keep Niko at further than an arm's length."

"And there's *my* daughter, shining though as well, thinking with her emotions," Victoria smiled. "But I see that you have placed the Prussians right next door at Clarence House. Isn't that a bit of a privilege for a family we have no close ties to?"

"Ah, Mama, but they are extraordinarily important to nearly all of their neighboring countries. The King is working on almost nothing other than his plans to unify the German states. From the looks of things, he might just be successful one day. I doubt Austria will ever go along, but he and his brother seem to have the power to bully the other German states into it. Anyhow, I am sure the King would see it as a slight if any of the other states were placed ahead of him, with the exception of our close family, of course."

"When did you become so well-versed in foreign affairs?" her mother marveled.

"Mama, you receive newspapers from all over the continent every day. Who do you think reads them, the staff?"

"Yes, you are your father's daughter," the queen remarked dryly. The truth was Victoria had totally forgotten all the newspaper subscriptions the Palace received. That had been something Albert set up that she never paid enough attention to discontinue.

Returning to her plans, Vicky pointed out, "As you can see I have also placed the Danes at Clarence. They are in a bitter dispute with Prussia about the future of the Duchies of Schleswig-Holstein. As it was Britain that helped them reach the *London Accord* to solve the last crisis there, I am hoping being in London again, will give them the boost to resolve the issue a little more amicably a second time. Also, the new Danish crown prince has a daughter who, though a bit young still, might make a good match for Prince Fritz to further cement a peaceful connection between the two counties."

"This is the Fritz you were so taken with in Brussels?"

"Yes it is. I do so wish he wasn't destined to be a king himself one day. That would make this husband shopping business so much simpler."

"Very clever, dear. Maybe all of us old matriarchs should just sit back and let you do the matchmaking for us."

"You're not old, Mama. You're not even forty yet."

"You are the second person to remind that today. Maybe I should start believing it."

"Who was the first?"

"John Brown," the queen said simply.

"Seems to be an odd choice to be discussing your age with."

"Sweetheart, like you, my birth was announced with cannon fire. It's not exactly a secret when I was born."

"Still, I would not have expected you to have that type of conversation with the staff is all."

"But surely you talk about such things with Louisa?"

"That's a little different, she is also a close friend."

"Mr. Brown is quickly becoming a close friend, as well."

CHAPTER 10

"So tonight's the big night." Billy said it more as a statement than a question.

"Yes, tonight is a beginning of the rest of my life," Vicky said rather morosely.

Vicky was taking her morning walk through the gardens of Buckingham Palace. It was a fairly brisk November morning, but the sky was clear with just a few fluffy clouds here and there. She had made a habit of taking a daily stroll any morning the weather permitted. It helped clear her head and organize the rest of her day. As with anytime she left the confines of the Palace, even onto its own balconies and grounds, she had Billy Saint Albans in tow, officially as her personal protection, but more often as a sounding board for various ideas she had.

"Not entirely," he responded. "Your mother only expects you to *pick* a future husband tonight. I would imagine the engagement will not be announced until the New Year, and the wedding itself wouldn't be until next summer, at the earliest."

"It will be June 5th. Mama has already written it into her calendar. Now it's just a matter of filling the blank for the groom's name. After that, the rest is mostly orchestrated."

"Isn't that what tonight is supposed to do?"

"That's Mama's plan. I'm not so sure I'm ready for that. And the choices are so limited."

"Are you absolutely sure it has to be a *foreign* prince?" Billy asked tentatively.

"Well, there aren't any eligible British ones about anymore, so I guess it does. Not that I'm all that fond of my English cousins anyway. They are just too ... too ... Hanoverian for my taste."

"I get it. You want a quieter man who won't be gallivanting all over."

"That would be ideal, but I think I'm stuck with a 'gallivanter'."

"You mean the Oldenburg Duke."

"Yes, I don't see marriage settling him down that much."

"Then your mind is made up on him?" The disappointment was obvious in Billy's voice, though Vicky either didn't notice or chose not to let on that she had.

"I don't see that I have much of a choice. He is literally the only eligible bachelor who is royal, not going to be king himself someday, an adult, and not closer to my mother's age than my own."

"You know, there is nothing written that you have to marry a royal. Look at Uncle Jimmy. He married Anne Hyde, whose father wasn't even noble yet."

"Uncle Jimmy? You mean James II? I'm not sure one of England's few deposed kings is a glowing recommendation."

"But it wasn't because of Anne. He got bounced because his second wife, the royal wife, convinced him to convert to join the papists."

"True, but some historians question if his marriage to Anne was even legal *because* it was to a commoner."

"Both of her daughters became Queen themselves, so that seems pretty legal to me."

"I guess." By now Vicky had paused her walk and peered over a waist-high brick fence that divided the Palace's boundary from the field used by the Royal Mews. She liked watching the horses eat and frolic about without a care in the world. She envied them on days like today. "But James only had to get permission from his brother Charles II, not exactly the world's authority on propriety. I have to get permission from Gloriana personified."

"Might she settle for a semi-royal?" Vicky suddenly felt Billy's hands lightly on her shoulders. She was shocked but made herself not flinch. His touch was light, gentle, the softest of caresses. She turned, intending to remind him his place, but as soon as they were face-to-face, he kissed her. Not the hungry, sensual way Niko has once kissed her, which resulted in him getting slapped. But light, apprehensive, as if seeking permission. She allowed herself three seconds to savor the feeling, but then gently broke it off.

"What do think you are doing?" She tried to sound like she was reprimanding, but it came out sounding much more like "Why only now?" in tone.

"After tonight, you are determined to belong to someone else. I just wanted to be clear there is another choice. You only have to choose it."

"The Queen would never approve. The government would never let her."

"Parliament has no say in the matter. And your mother might be more amenable than you think. After all, she is a woman who experienced great love once, and not for your father's title."

"We need to get back, there is much to do before tonight." Vicky strode off at a pace that prevented Billy from continuing. But she suspected this was not the end of the conversation.

***

"Well, this is it." Vicky said for about the third time as she breathed deeply to calm her nerves once more.

"You'll be fine," Louie assured her.

"But how do I pick a husband from this lot?"

"Okay, let's be a little realistic, here." Louie had about enough of Vicky's refusal to see the answer staring her so blatantly in the face. "We both know there is only one logical choice here. You have eliminated everyone else because of their age, their religion, or their unavailability. So, just go out there and dance with whomever you want to, knowing at the end of the night you will end up with Duke Nicholas."

"But he is so...so...immature," Vicky sputtered.

"All the better, he's not set in his ways, so you can mold him into the consort you want him be."

"Am I a potter or a princess?"

"When it comes to husbands, you're both."

"Is it too late to feign illness?"

"Yes, it is!" Queen Victoria answered before Louie could. Neither lady had noticed the queen walk up behind them. "Come along child, we shall enter together," Her Majesty commanded.

"No turning back now!" Vicky quickly whispered before taking her position at the Queen's right side, but a step behind her. "Good evening, Mr. Brown," Vicky acknowledged the queen's servant who was just behind them on the left. He merely bowed his head to her. Vicky noted how odd that he would be here. This position was usually taken by a lady in waiting, but she was further back.

The doors were opened by footmen and the royal procession entered.

***

By midnight, Vicky had danced with nearly every prince in the place. The one she had avoided was Niko, which was easy since he ignored her, too. For his part, he seemed to be having a grand time swinging all the eligible princesses around the room. Vicky occupied her mind with other matters in an effort to not notice him.

One major accomplishment of the night was to suggest to Prince Fritz of Prussia a potential solution to a particularly tricky political issue, the "Holstein Problem". It was well-known that Prince Fritz's father and uncle were working towards the creation of a German Empire. While there were several internal German issues to resolve, one of the larger foreign stumbling blocks was the Duchy of Schleswig-Holstein which sat on the border with Denmark.

It was actually two separate duchies ruled by a common duke. Both were closely associated by history and family to the Danish Throne and were about to become even more closely connected. The second son of the duke had recently been selected to succeed the Danish King who had no obvious heirs. The problem arises in that Holstein's population is predominantly German, while Schleswig's is Danish. Prussia wanted to annex all of Schleswig-Holstein as part of its imperial plan, but Denmark has resisted. Two plebiscites on the question have been inconclusive with each of the portions of the dual duchy voting opposite ways.

Vicky's solution was to transfer the Duchy of Holstein to the person of new Crown Prince of Denmark's eldest daughter, Alexandra. This would keep it within the Schleswig-Holstein family as she is the niece of the current Duke, and therefore would meet the requirements of the constitution and various existing treaties. Alexandra would then marry Prince Fritz, bringing Holstein into the German Empire by inheritance rather than by annexation. In the future, Holstein would then be an autonomous duchy within the German Empire, if such were ever achieved, and Schleswig was free to remain a protectorate of Denmark.

After having a couple of dances with the young Princess Alexandra, Fritz found this solution to be absolutely what was needed. His father was not immediately sold on the idea, but Fritz's mother, her own marriage the product of a peace treaty, assured

Fritz she would work on her husband and on the King, his brother. Alexandra was still underage so there was still time to work out the details.

Having resolved that thorny mess, Vicky soon found herself being swirled and twirled by the Russian Tsar, who was in attendance with his elder son the Tsarevich Nicholas and the Grand Duke Alexander, two and four years younger than Vicky respectively.

"You are just as lovely and light on your feet as you mother was at your age," the Tsar was saying. "Did you know I was quite taken with her on my first trip to England?"

"Mama mentioned you coming here when you were tsarevich, and how handsome you were in your Hussars uniform."

"I'm sure twenty years has reduced that image a might."

"You are still a very handsome man, and also quite a good dancer as well."

"It would seem my cousin Niko has no problems on the dance floor either, eh?"

"I wouldn't know. Her has yet to ask me to dance tonight."

"He will, he will. He knows his future lies here in England. I think he is just sampling the rest of Europe before he makes his way over here."

"Well, he certainly has many more choices than I do, that's for sure. It seems I was born in the midst of an epidemic of princesses, but very few princes."

"Mon cherie, you only need one. And Niko is such a perfect fit for you. I have long desired to strengthen the ties between our two realms, but there has not been a proper combination to make such an alignment, until now. And the timing could not be more beneficial. What better way to transition to a time of peace after my father's ill-advised adventure in Crimea? I will be so happy to welcome you to St Petersburg after your marriage, for a visit, of course. I know your duty lies here."

"You sound as if an engagement has already been announced. I have not even received a proposal, yet."

"Formalities, my dear. Perhaps I am putting the troika in front of the horses, but your mother made it sound as if all was decided and only the announcements needed to be made."

"Mama's horses seem to be running a bit wild themselves," Vicky said as she looked over at the Queen dancing with her servant, John Brown. As more people realized what was happening, nearly all dancing stopped as the whole room looked on at the spectacle. It was considered quite a breach of protocol for a servant to be on the dance floor at all, but dancing with the queen? That was rapidly approaching scandalous.

Thinking quickly, Vicky excused herself from her own partner, and grabbing Louie by the hand, hastened over to Niko. "Don't ask, just dance," she ordered both of them. Then she quickly went to his post just inside the door and dragged Billy onto the dance floor with her. As Billy began to move her around the ballroom, she looked about until she caught the eye of Fitz of Prussia. Jerking her head towards the raised dais, he nodded his understanding and walked over casually to ask the Queen's lady-in-waiting to dance.

Once the gasping came to an end, several of the guests, although perplexed at what they assumed to be an odd British tradition, returned to the dance floor themselves and the ball carried on as before. When that piece of music ended, the Queen returned to her makeshift Throne on the dais, with Mr. Brown taking up his usual position just behind her. They were joined by the lady-in-waiting while Billy took up his position guarding the doorway and Louie joined Vicky near the same exit.

"What on Earth just happened?" asked Louie.

"I have no idea, but now is not the time to find out. I'll discuss it with Mama tomorrow. Thank you both helping make it as less awkward as possible."

"He really is a good dancer, you know." Louie pointed out.

"I know. I was a little surprised at how well Billy dances."

"Not Billy, you ninny. Niko."

"Well, he does seem rather athletic, so I should not be surprised."

"So, when are you going to dance with him and find out for yourself?"

"He hasn't asked me to dance yet. But after that last little adventure, I think I need to get some air first. You remain here and let anyone looking for me know I will be back shortly." As she walked through the exit, "Capt. Saint Albans, I am going out or some air."

Responding to his cue, he followed her down the corridor to an exit which led onto a balcony overlooking the palace gardens.

"Are you having a good time tonight?" he asked when they were away from the doors and to a quiet place where they could talk.

"For the most part I am, despite Mama's apparent bout of spontaneity. Most of the men here are leaders of their nations and it has been great talking to them about the issues going on in each of their countries."

"I couldn't help but notice there is one man you have not danced with."

"If you are referring to Duke Nicholas, he has not asked me to dance. At least, not yet. He seems to be content with the princesses who have more, how should I say this? Let's call it less on their mind."

"Or perhaps simply less mind?" Billy offered.

They both laughed. Vicky enjoyed these off-the-cuff chats with Billy. They had developed a comfortable nature between them. She knew he was smitten with her, and she was a bit taken with him too. She thought they both understood it could go nowhere, so they could just be themselves. But Vicky sensed something different tonight. While they could always relax in each other's company when no one else was around, Billy knew his position and didn't move out of it. But tonight he maneuvered himself so that he was in front of her.

"Billy, what are you doing?"

The next thing she knew, he was on one knee in front of her. "I know you believe it is not allowed, but I have consulted with the Clerk of the Lords on the matter, and he can see no legal reason why a princess cannot marry a Peer of the Realm. Therefore, Your Royal Highness, I pledge my eternal love and devotion to you and to the Kingdom, will you accept me as your consort?"

"Billy, I ... I can't. Mama will never approve."

"You don't know that unless you ask her."

"She's already informed the Tsar of Russia that she is expecting me to marry his cousin, Duke Niko. And I think the Tsar has told everyone else. He is already talking about alliances between our two nations and cementing peace after the recent war."

"But do you love him?"

"What?"

"Do you love Niko?"

She could not answer immediately. She had been asking herself this very question ever since their little adventure in Brussels. She could not deny there was a strong physical attraction between them, but how did she *feel* about him? For that, she yet to form an answer. For now, she fell back on what she had been telling herself all along, "I'm a princess, what does love have to do with it?"

"Everything! I love you, Vicky, and I suspect you love me too."

"Is it love? I do feel very fond of you, but is it love? I don't know. How could I? I've only started meeting men."

"But it's more than you feel for that Hun!" Billy blurted out.

"How do you know how I feel, when I'm not sure myself."

Billy stood up and looked directly into Vicky's face. "Look me in the eye and tell me you are prepared to spend the rest of your life with that man, have children with him, eventually reign with him at your side."

She could not. Looking down, she simply said, "I'm not prepared for that with any man."

"Then tell your mother *that*. I'm not going anywhere. I'll wait for you, until you *are* ready...will he?"

Vicky remembered about what the Tsar said about Niko sampling the rest of Europe. Was he making a back-up plan in case she said no? If she asked him to wait, would he? Probably not. He was already showing signs of impatience. But there was that one thing she could never admit to Billy. She could hardly admit to herself. Niko ignited a fire in her she could suppress, but not deny. When she slept at night, it might have been Billy's soothing voice she heard in her dreams, but it was Niko's near-naked body standing in that pond in Brussels that she saw.

"He is going to have to," she finally said. "Billy, I do care for you. But, I have a duty to perform. It's not even as if I had anyone to pass it off onto. I have no siblings, the next heir after me is a foreign king. I have to put the Crown first."

"Are you at least going to tell him he has to wait too?"

"I will, assuming I ever get the chance to talk to him. He was been clearly avoiding me so far tonight. I am not sure why."

"Well, this is your ball. You could seek him out."

"Okay, you got me. I've been avoiding him, too. But I guess I can't any longer. I'll talk to both him and mother as soon as the chance arises. But for now, we have to get back in there."

Billy escorted her back to the ballroom, taking up his guard duty position, just inside the door. Vicky started across the room toward her mother's chair. She vaguely noticed the music had momentarily stopped as the performers were catching their breath before continuing. The guests were standing around merely chatting to one another. Halfway across the room, she suddenly found herself face-to-face with Niko.

"May I have this dance, Your Royal Highness?" he asked very formally, bowing at the waist. Vicky had no option but to curtsy and accept his hand. Louie was right, he did dance marvelously. Vicky imagined anything that required physical ability was probably easy for Niko. She felt herself blushing as her mind went to what those physical abilities could include.

"So what was that about with ordering me to dance with your maid?"

"I'm not sure yet. I'll have to ask my mother about it later. I hope she did not make too much of a spectacle of herself. That's the last thing that needs to be in tomorrow's papers."

"Don't worry, my dear. I am sure they will have other things to discuss."

As Vicky and Niko waltzed around the room, she noticed more and more dancers were exiting the dancefloor. Soon, they were only couple dancing. Vicky listened to be sure the music was still playing just when it stopped abruptly. Niko also stopped abruptly, throwing Vicky a little off-balance. Luckily, the long gown covered her feet wobbling as she regained her balance, partially by hanging on to Niko. Just as suddenly, Vicky was experiencing déjà vu when Niko dropped to one knee in the middle of the ball room, in front of all of those assembled, including the Queen.

Bowing first to the Queen, "Your Majesty, I humbly request your consent for The Princess Royal's hand in matrimony." Then turned back to Vicky, "Your Royal Highness, would you do me the extreme honor of consenting to be my bride?"

Vicky was so shocked, she stood perfectly still. This was *not* the way this should be happening. She intended to tell her mother she had to wait. Now, in front of essentially all of Europe, she had been denied the opportunity to request a pause. It was either yes or no. She looked down into those pools of sky blue eyes and could not help but think his thin mustache so perfectly matched his face. And his dark brown wavy hair, worn just below his collar, encircled his head like a halo.

Then her thoughts went to the other person she had looked at like this tonight. Billy was such a sweet, reliable man. The perfect man to be a husband and father. She could see Billy teaching their children how to dress, how to act. Could she count on this popinjay even being there for their children? Why can't Billy be royal? Why can't Billy be this beautiful? He was a handsome man, but Niko's beauty was the kind that sucked the very air from a room. Maybe she was assuming too much about Billy. After all, she had never seen him without clothes like she had Niko. Could he be hiding more than she knew under those fancy uniforms?

Stop it! She became aware everyone was waiting for a response, hanging on her every word, well any word. *Say something!*

She closed her eyes for a second, took in a breath, and breathed it back out, whispering "Yes." as she did.

CHAPTER 11

Vicky managed to continue with the evening, but only in a surreal fog. She danced the rest of the evening exclusively with Niko while he prattled on about nothing important. She avoided even looking in Billy's direction. *How could have I betrayed him like that? I told him I would make Niko wait.*

After what she deemed to an appropriate amount of time to receive the well wishes of the other guests, and what seemed an eternity to her, Vicky made her excuses of needing to sleep and retired from the ball with Louie in tow. Even then she managed to leave the ballroom with her head down so she wouldn't have to look at Billy's face. It was Louie who advised him they were in for the evening so his services were not needed anymore that night.

Once back in her own room she told Louie about Billy's proposal and her promise to him. Once out of her ball gown and able to sit comfortably in front of a roaring fireplace, she was able to seek her advice.

"Oh Louie, what have I done?" Vicky bemoaned.

"Nothing less than what was expected of you. Although, it might have been a bit unfair springing it on you in the middle of the dance floor like that," she conceded.

"But I promised Billy I going to make Niko wait. He wanted time to make his case to Mama."

"Do you love him?" Louie asked point blank.

"Who?"

"Billy, of course."

"No... well, maybe...I don't know!" Vicky was on the point of tears at this point.

"Well then, do you love Niko?"

"Maybe? I don't know that either!"

"You're not making this any easier," Louie looked at the princess skeptically. "Well, you said yourself you mother is planning the wedding in June, that is over six months away. I suggest you figure it out before then. There is nothing more to be done tonight. You are exhausted, get some sleep." With that Louie got Vicky all tucked into bed and excused herself for the night.

Vicky tried to sleep, but each time she managed to doze off, she kept dreaming of Billy and Niko each grabbing an arm and pulling her in opposite directions. She was afraid she would rip like a ragdoll. Just as she felt herself tearing in half, she would wake. Sleep did not come back easily after each dream.

*** *

Niko's prediction was correct. The newspapers did not take much notice of the queen's unorthodox dance with John Brown. The headline, in the largest possible lettering, rang out the news, "PRINCESS ENGAGED."

The remainder of the page was covered with large separate portraits of Duke Nicholas of Oldenburg and the Princess Royal, and a detailed account of the evening's festivities.

"Well, that's a bit unexpected," John Stockley said to himself. "A bit young if you ask me, but then you didn't, didja?" John took another swig of his mid-morning mead. "I guess somethin' is gonna have to be done about this. We can't have you burdenin' us with another generation of royal brats."

***

Breakfast the morning after a ball was almost close to being a luncheon. Vicky and her mother arrived at the table almost simultaneously. Being the first time she encountered the Queen that day, Vicky curtsied to her before taking her seat.

"Good morning, Mama, I would have expected you to already come down. Did you have as much trouble sleeping as I did?"

"Good morning, dear. No, once I got to sleep I slept quite soundly, but I'm afraid I was up later than was good for me."

"Then the ball went on for some time after I left?"

"No. not really. It pretty much wound down from there. But I had a few other things to handle before going to bed." The queen seemed quite intent on changing the subject. "So was excitement at your prospective wedding keeping you awake?"

"I'm not sure I would call it excitement, as much as terror."

"Oh, don't let those nerves get to you. I was just as scared when your father asked to marry me."

"I don't even think I have gotten to *that* set of fears, yet. I'm more afraid I betrayed someone by accepting Niko's proposal so quickly."

"Quickly," the Queen tutted. "You took so long to answer, I thought you were going to do something foolish like say No."

"That was my intention," Vicky confessed.

"But why would you do that? There really weren't any other choices there for you."

"Not exactly say 'no', but more of a 'not yet'. Mama, I don't feel like I'm ready to marry anyone yet."

"Nonsense, sweetheart. You are only a year younger than I was when I got married. Your fears will settle as the time comes closer, you'll see," the queen advised.

"But there was actually another choice I could have made." Vicky spelled out to her mother everything that had transpired between her and Billy.

"I see. The most important question right now is do you love Saint Albans?"

"I don't know."

"Well, do you love Niko?"

"I don't know that either."

"My dear, the first thing you need to go then is figure that part out. And since the whole world now thinks you are marrying the one duke, I strongly suggest you give him ample consideration!" The queen got up from her seat, clearly in a huff.

"But Mama, you hardly touched your breakfast." Vicky wanted more than anything for her mother to sit with her and help her decide what to do.

"I think I have had quite enough this morning. I need to go to my office and get some work done," she snipped and stormed off.

"That went well." Vicky rolled her eyes before losing her own appetite and leaving the table also.

***

Vicky spent the next two days in her room, refusing to see anyone other than allowing Louie to bring her food, of which she ate very little. Niko made a couple of requests to see her but was informed she was unwell. The same excuse fended off the person she was most avoiding, Billy, as well.

By the third day, she couldn't stand the sight of her bedroom any longer and finally got up and re-entered the world. Thankfully, the rain of the past few days had let up and she would be able to take one of her morning walks. This would give her a chance to apologize to Billy.

After breakfast, she dressed in her boots and long coat. The rain might have stopped, but there was still a chill in the air and the fog was being slow to burn off. During her self-imposed quarantine, she had received a gift from her fiancé. It was a fur-trimmed Russian-style hat, the perfect thing to keep her ears warm on a day like today.

Before she went down, Louie finally spoke up. "There is something you need to know before you go outside," she told Vicky. She took a deep breath and said quickly, "Billy has been re-assigned. You have not been assigned a new permanent bodyguard yet. The

Guards have been taking it in turns, so I don't know the man who will escort you today."

"Re-assigned? To where? Why?"

"I haven't been told, but I heard one of the cleaning maids say he was very upset the morning after the ball."

"She sacked him!" Vicky exclaimed. "I told Mama that Billy had also proposed to me, and she got angry. She probably sent him off to India, or worse, darkest Africa!" Without another word, she ran all the way to her mother's office.

The queen was working at her desk not really paying much attention when Vicky stormed in the private entrance, giving Victoria quite the start. "Whatever is wrong, child?"

"You sacked Billy!" Vicky accused. "I tried to tell him. I knew the establishment would have never let me marry him. But to send him away? There was no need for that!"

"Vicky, Vicky, calm down," her mother begged.

"Where has he gone?"

"Well, I don't know. That would be for his commanding officer to decide."

"I don't believe you, Mother." Vicky almost never called the queen "Mother" except when she was angry with her. "Where did you send him?"

"Remember who you are talking to, young lady," Victoria reprimanded as she stood up to face her daughter, though even standing she still had to look up to look at Vicky in the face. "I have no idea where Capt. Saint Albans has been reassigned because I did not ask him to leave. He came to me and confessed his feelings for you. He told me himself he had proposed, but you accepted Oldenburg's hand instead. Under the circumstances, he felt he could not protect you in a dispassionate manner, especially in your fiancé's presence so he asked to be reassigned. And since you have been acting like a scared little girl hiding in your room, Col. Everton-Smythe has not been able to present any candidates for your approval for a replacement. So, if you are quite done with your hysterics, perhaps you could see your way clear to set up appointments to select a new guard."

"He chose to leave?" Vicky asked heart-broken.

"Well, I'm glad something I said got through!" the queen exclaimed. "Saint Albans left this letter for you, for when you were ready to read it." Victoria handed her daughter the letter.

The first thing Vicky noticed is that it was still sealed with a wax seal including an engraving of the arms of the Dukes of Saint Albans. "Thank you, Mama," Vicky said in defeated voice. "I'm going to go for a walk and try to clear my head. When I get back, I'll address whatever duties I've neglected the past few days."

"Wise course of action," the queen said and reclaimed her seat. "The guard of the moment is stationed at the door. Take him with you."

"Of course," Vicky responded absently.

Vicky left her mother's office, putting on her hat and coat again that Louie had been holding while waiting outside the office door.

As she approached the door to the courtyard, the first thing she noticed was the very un-military manner in which her guard de jure was squatting with his arms relaxing on his knees. As soon as he saw the princess, he jumped up to attention, but with nowhere near the sharpness, Vicky had come to expect. But then, everything about the guard seemed to be the opposite of Billy. Where Billy had a trim physique, this man was verging on overweight, his tunic barely concealing what was obviously an extended gut. And while he was shaved, bits of stubble were still clearly visible along his jaw line. But she had to have a guard to go outside, so he would have to do. She only hoped he could keep up with her brisk walk.

"Please attend me as I walk about the grounds," Vicky asked as she walked past the man, not stopping for a reply.

The guard hung back a little further than she was used to, but she was okay with that. She really wanted her space at the moment. What she really wanted was a quiet place to read the letter from Billy which she clung to as made a bee line for the fence where she liked to watch the horses.

The ground was still soggy from nonstop rain the past two days. The nip in the air told her snow was not far away. Once at the fence, she stopped with her guard a few paces behind her. He said nothing, looking around in silence, and she was not up for a conversation with a stranger either. She broke the seal on the letter and opened it to find a short note in precise, quite masculine, tightly formed perfect penmanship:

Your Royal Highness,

What happened to waiting?

I guess it doesn't matter now. You made your choice. Now I have to make mine.

I can't bear to watch you two as you grow closer and eventually become man and wife, then parents. I need a little distance, so I have taken a leave of absence from the Home Guard to return to Nottingham to oversee the operation of my family's estate there.

I hope you will be happy,

Your obedient and humble servant,
Saint Albans.

The first thing Vicky noticed was the formality of both the salutation and the signature. No Vicky and Billy anymore, apparently. She felt the tears build on her eyelids. She blinked them away best she could. She was very conscious there was a stranger with her and did not wish for him to see her become all emotional. To busy her hands, her removed the fur cap she had received as a gift from Niko just that morning. She thought that Russia must indeed be very cold for this heavy thing to be practical. Perhaps she should save it to when she inevitably visited there.

Not being terribly successful at clearing the tears from her eyes she did not notice her bodyguard moving closer until it was too late. She had almost no time to react when his hand covered her mouth. In her last seconds of consciousness, she stuffed Billy's letter into the furry hat and felt is escape her grasp.

CHAPTER 12

Louie started to become anxious when Vicky did not return. She checked often at the door to the courtyard and the guard who was normally there solely for the princess' use was nowhere to be seen. She even went so far as to go out onto the balcony overlooking the gardens to see if she could see her mistress. But there were many places she could not see from there, any of which Vicky could have chosen for part of her walk.

Just as she decided to make the bolder move of donning a coat and going to look for her, Col. Everton-Smythe and a whole squadron of guards came racing into the palace. Louie followed them to see the colonel assign guards to different doors, finally taking the rest with him to the queen's office. They were obviously concerned about something specific, so she followed them.

As she passed a set of windows facing out on the front public entrance area to the palace, she saw it flooded with a mixture of the Home Guard along with several members of the regular army's 13th Battalion, whose garrison was nearby.

Everton-Smythe sent one guard to stand outside the private family entrance to the queen's office and assigned another to guard to more formal entrance. By this point, Louie caught up to the colonel. "Col. Everton-Smythe!" she called out to him. "What is happening?"

"Who are you, my lady?" the colonel was astute to recognize immediately Louie was dressed too properly to be a servant.

"I'm the Princess Royal's lady-in-waiting, the Lady Louisa Howard" Louie responded, rather annoyed the colonel did not remember her. They had already met at various functions several times.

"Oh yes, of course, forgive me, do you know where Her Royal Highness is at the moment?"

"She went for a walk and has not returned."

"Has she been gone long?"

"Long enough that I was about to start looking for her."

"Oh my god," the blood drained from the colonel's face. He turned to one of the guards with him and ordered an immediate and thorough search of the entire grounds.

"She does have a guard with her. She never leaves the building of the Palace without one. Until recently it would have Lt. Saint Albans, but since he has left, I'm not sure who it was."

"Well that might be good news... I hope. Come with me, we must speak with the Queen immediately, and you might have pertinent information for us." He did not elaborate further and turned to head towards the office.

Upon arriving, Charles Grey looked up in surprise. "How may I help you, Colonel?"

"I must see the Queen at once, it is extremely urgent."

"One moment." Charles knocked softly on the office door and then entered. A moment later he returned, opening the door widely. "You may enter."

Everton-Smythe assigned the two remaining guards to stand watch outside the office, giving one the instruction to rotate between this position and that of the private entrance. "And as you move about keep your eyes open! Challenge any guard you do not personally know on a first name basis!" he ordered.

By now, Louie was frightened, actually on the verge of being truly scared. She followed the colonel into see the Queen. Once inside the office she stopped to curtsy as the colonel bowed his head quickly then moved on.

"Colonel, what is this all about?" Victoria asked.

"Your Majesty, I have reason to believe there is an intruder in the Palace disguised as a Home Guard officer. I have my men searching thoroughly through both the building and the grounds and have borrowed some regular army from the local garrison to secure the perimeter."

"What has led to all of this?" the Queen asked.

"We found the body of one of our guards hidden in some bushes on the grounds. He had been murdered and his uniform was stolen."

"Oh my goodness," the Queen exclaimed. Louie sucked in a deep breath herself but managed to remain silent.

"I'm afraid there is more. The dead guard was one of the men assigned to the rotation to guard the Princess Royal."

The Queen blanched, looked about a moment as if looking for something, then seeing the lady-in-waiting standing there, too scared to keep up protocol, asked, "Louie, where is Vicky now?"

"She went for her usual morning walk, Ma'am."

"And you do not attend her on these walks?" the colonel asked.

"No, she prefers to not have to talk to anyone. It is her 'quiet time' to think, as she calls it."

Just then there was a knock at the door and the private secretary entered.

"What is it, Charles?" the Queen almost snapped at him.

"Colonel, one of your men says he needs to speak you urgently."

"If I may, Ma'am?" the colonel looked towards the Queen.

"Of course," she uttered absently. Everton-Smythe backed out the Queen's presence.

"Louie, how long has my daughter been on this walk of hers?"

"Over an hour now, Ma'am."

"Is she usually gone this long?"

"No Ma'am, I just on my way to start looking for her when the guards came running in."

Everton-Smythe rejoined to the two ladies with a grave look on his face. He was holding what appeared to be a ball of fur in his hands.

"Ma'am," he addressed the Queen. "My men found a spot out by the fence between the grounds and Royal Mews where an apparent struggle occurred."

"That is one of Vick...er, the princess' favorite places to visit. She likes to watch the horses," Louie offered.

"They found this on the ground there." He held up the Russian style hat, and as he did, a letter fell out. The Queen recognized it immediately as the one she had handed her daughter only a short while ago.

"VICKY!"

***

The first sensation to come to Vicky was the coldness of her face. As she groggily fought off the effects of the ether used to subdue her, she came to realize she was laying on a bed and was covered by a heavy blanket. In a moment of panic, she thought she tied to the bed, but as she flailed about, the blanket fell off and she realized she was only held down by its weight. She also quickly knew why: the room was very cold.

Sitting up, she peered around the mostly darkened room. It was bare except for the cot she was on and a small table in the far corner. The table had no chairs but did have a single candle burning on it, the only source of light as there were no windows. The wall next to the cot was brick, but the other three walls appeared to be wood. There was a single, rather small, door.

She got up and went to the door. It was made of a thick wood and would not budge as she pushed on it. There was no doorknob. She cried out "Hello?" and waited but heard nothing. She called again, "Is anyone there?" but was met with the same absolute silence.

127

"What do you want with me?" she screamed as she pounded the door. When no answer came, she sat back on the bed.

Soon the cold started settling in so she wrapped up in the thick blanket, which appeared to be made from an animal hide of some kind. One side was furry, but the bottom side was a simple linen material. It felt like it had been filled with perhaps down. It was very warm.

Vicky's brain was flooded with rapid questions, none of which she could answer. *Why am I here? Where is here? Who did this? Am I going to die?* She ran her hands through her hair in fear. That was when she noticed her hair only went to her neck. The rest was gone.

CHAPTER 13

John Thadeus Delane was an attentive man. He had quite the eye for detail. This had done him well in his career as a newspaperman. Now, as Editor of *The Times* these past seventeen years, he used this gift to make sure every story in his paper was correct, from being fully verified to perfectly proofread.

Therefore, he wasn't even all the way into his office when he noticed the puffy envelope sitting on his desk. As he walked around the enormous mahogany alter which consumed more than its fair share of the office, the envelope, small and ordinary in every way looked a little like a small rowboat floating in an ocean. Somehow, Delane knew this small vessel, addressed simply THE EDITOR, and with no return address, was going to unleash a storm when opened.

Using his ornate nacre handled letter opener, he sliced through the top of the envelope and pulled out the contents. Before unfolding the letter, he saw a braid of dark hair and a square of material land in the sea that was his desktop.

"This doesn't look good," he muttered to himself and unfolded the single sheet of paper, the penmanship of the note was in same deliberate slowly printed block capital letters as had been used on the outside of the envelope:

I HAVE THE PRINCESS.
TELL YOUR FRIENDS IN WESTMINSTER
I HAVE ONE DEMAND:
END THE MONARCHY AND DECLARE A
REPUBLIC. PRINT THEIR REPLY ON THE
FRONT PAGE.
I WON'T ASK TWICE

***

Vicky woke up confused. She did not remember drifting off to sleep between her sobs. She was still sitting on the cot in her little cell, her neck sore from sleeping while sitting up. As she stretched, she noticed it was warmer than before. That was when she saw the door was open.

Walking into the outer room, she quickly went to the closed door on the other side. It was closed just as securely as the door to the inner cold room had been earlier. Again there were no windows, but this room had wood walls on all sides. Vicky quickly tested the walls, but they were substantial and gave no indication of being thin when she knocked on them.

The source of the heat in this room was a pot-belled stove near one of the outer walls with a little pile of wood next to it. The warmth it provided was enough for comfort in both rooms, as long as the door between them was kept open. In the center was a table with two chairs. It was a rather plain table, but adequate to place a small meal on and eat from. On the table was a plate with some bread and cheese and a small pitcher of water. *Thankfully, he does not mean to starve me.* Vicky thought. *Though if this is his idea of a full meal, I might get a little thinner.*

In one corner of the room was a chamber pot with a lid. After several minutes hesitation, her physical needs overrode her concern he might walk in and her general disgust at the notion of using it, but there was no water closet here. At least she was familiar with such things from being ill as a child and having to use one next to her bed when not being allowed to walk as far as the water closet down the hall from her bedroom.

After relieving her bladder and returning the pot's lid, she sat at the table to eat the meagre meal left for her. Because there were no windows, and she had no idea how long she had slept, she could not even determine if it was night or day. Was this luncheon? Dinner? Did it matter?

While she picked at the bread and cheese, she further accessed her situation. *What does this man want? Is it just that fake guard, or is this part of a larger plot?* Vicky, always a rather bright girl, had already come to the conclusion the guard who grabbed her on her walk was not a real member of the Home Guard. That was why his uniform looked not quite right, and his hair seemed a bit unkempt. *Of course,* she scolded herself, *if you were really all that smart, you would not gone out with him alone, with those warning signs staring you in the face.*

The only thing that makes sense is he is holding me for ransom. If he intended to kill me he would have done so in the gardens and not bothered with the trouble of bringing me here, wherever here is. In that case, I should be freed as soon as Mama pays.

Not having anything in the room to spend her attention on, all she could do is think. And the only thing, besides her current predicament, that she could think about was the anguished letter from Billy. She hoped her kidnapper had not bothered to pick up her hat when he took her. Since it was not with her in this room, she was encouraged it, with the letter, was left behind to be found by a search party. It was all she could think to do as she was being grabbed, leave some sign that she was taken, and did not run off or anything.

The more she thought, the more she was comfortable with her ransom theory. That would explain why her braid of hair was missing. *He must have sent it as proof that he really had me. Louie would recognize the hair tie immediately as one of mine. And the torn piece missing from my dress; she would know it came from the one I was wearing this morning. This all makes sense. All I have to do is sit patiently and once he gets his money, he'll let me go. I hope.*

Does Billy know this is all happening? The thought came to her, followed immediately by a less welcome one. *Will he care? I guess he thinks I'm Niko's problem now. How is Niko responding to all of this?* She realized she had no idea how he would react. She never saw him take anything seriously. Would he be able to handle a serious situation like this? Surely serious issues would come up once they were married, that was just life. Could he take them seriously? She knew Billy would.

That's not fair! She reprimanded herself. *You can't continue to compare them. Niko is the man in your life now, and Billy ... Billy is not.* The thought of Billy being gone for good started the tears again. She went back to the bed and sobbed into the lone pillow she had been provided.

***

Billy Saint Albans couldn't think of one blasted reason to get out of bed. He didn't have a job to go to. He didn't have Vicky to go to. He could only imagine how she was spending her morning. Picking out floral arrangements for the wedding? Maybe a fitting for her wedding dress? Taking a stroll through the gardens with that Oldenburg Duke?

He'd only been in Nottingham for one night, yet London seemed to be a hazy dream already. Perhaps if he rolled over and went back to sleep, he could dream his way back there, back to Vicky. The knock at the door interrupted that thought. Rogers, the underbutler who was assigned to be his valet rather hastily yesterday when he showed up at Bestwood Lodge without prior notice, entered and opened the heavy curtains, flooding the room with sunlight.

"Bloody Hell!" Billy protested.

"I'm sorry, Your Grace, but the Duchess requests your presence at breakfast. She was rather insistent."

"It's fine, Rogers. I know what a bit....er...how my mother can be when she perceives things not going by her plan." Billy remembered, almost too late, that he was now in a house controlled by his formidable mother, a shrill woman on the best of days, and these were her servants. In all likelihood, anything he said would be reported back to her. "Inform Her Grace I will be down as soon as I clean up a bit and get dressed."

"Very good, sir."

Billy did not wait for Rogers to leave before getting out of bed. He didn't care if sleeping in the nude offended the make-shift valet or not. It would serve him right for blasting the sunlight in his face so early.

Once he splashed a bit of water on his hair to tame it, he quickly dressed, skipping shaving. He was off duty for the foreseeable future, so why not grow out his beard? When he arrived at the breakfast table he found his mother slathering jam on a scone, while his younger sisters, Diana and Charlotte, were serving themselves from the hot foods the servants offered.

"Oh there you are, Billy. I wasn't sure how long you be, so we were just starting without you."

"Good morning, Mother, Di, Lottie" Billy addressed his family as he filled his own plate with the sausages and eggs that were served.

"I hope you were able to get some rest last night. You seemed completely exhausted when you arrived yesterday."

"The trip from London was a bit trying. I can never seem to get comfortable on a train. And the roads between Nottingham and here are quite abysmal." Billy left off the part that he only got a couple of hours sleep, his mind dwelling on Vicky.

"Well, I am glad you have come for this visit," his mother started. "I have news that is better to tell you in person rather than by a letter."

"Oh?"

"I have found running this estate to be more than I can handle alone." She shot him a glance on the word "alone." She had not approved of him running off to London to play soldier, and never minced words about it. "Your sisters are a tremendous help, of course, but only with the house itself. The park and the mine have become simply too much." The Bestwood estate included one of England's largest coal mines.

"Isn't the land man, what's name, Shepherd? Isn't he handling all of that for you?"

"His name is Sheffield, and he does try, but I fear he is no longer up to the task. He's not a young man anymore, you know. Besides, he has never taken well to being ordered about by a woman."

"Perhaps you could 'order him about' a little less and simply let him do his job?" Billy suggested. His sisters, both in their teens, shoved food in their mouths to stifle their giggles.

"Your sarcasm has no place at the table, young man," his mother reprimanded sharply. "As I was saying, I need a man here on a more permanent basis to see to the business of the estate. Therefore, I have accepted the marriage proposal of Lord Falkland. We plan to marry in the spring once he has finished up some business in the colonies."

"Well, that is some news!" Billy exclaimed. "Is he returning to England permanently then?" Billy knew the 10th Viscount Falkland as the former Governor General of India where he continued on in various posts after his term ended some six years ago.

"Yes. The only reason I agreed to marry him is so he could take over the running of the estate here. You

135

obviously have no interest in it." The last bit was a stinging accusation, one which Billy could not deny. His interests were never in forestry or coal mining, the two industries that allowed his family to live quite comfortably and that built Bestwood Lodge.

Though called a "lodge," is was something of a cross between a castle and grand manor house. The original structure was built in the 14th century by Edward III, with several additions over the centuries since. It had been used as a royal hunting lodge until it was gifted to the first Duke of Saint Albans by his father, King Charles II.

"Well, I'm very happy you have someone to care for the estate and preserve it for your daughters and their future families." Billy winked as his sisters.

"And what of your future family?" his mother asked.

"If there is ever one, which at this moment I am doubting," Billy suddenly turned downcast, still dwelling on being rebuffed by his first and only love, "we will make do with the London townhome. I have a stronger disposition for city life, I'm afraid."

"Pshaw, you are far too young to dismiss marriage and family so easily. Besides, you must marry to keep the title going," his mother chastised.

"That is not nearly such as concern as you make it out. I have three uncles who all have several sons, and Uncle Amelius is still going. I received news recently that Aunt Fanny is pregnant, yet again."

"Yes, she is *expecting*," his mother stressed. "Such crude language is inappropriate at the table, and in front of your sisters. Remember, you're not with your army buddies here."

"It's the Palace Guard," he corrected, "but I do apologize," he said, notably to his sisters more so than his mother. They merely giggled and looked down. Clearly their mother had drilled into them not to speak unless asked a question directly. "But the point remains, there are plenty of heirs for my dukedom. I daresay I am blessed more than Her Majesty in that regard."

"That poor lady, I cannot even imagine the horror she is going through," the duchess said. "I will pray for her and her daughter constantly."

"Praying for them is admirable, but why? Has something happened?" Billy was suddenly concerned.

"Of course, you have not heard the news because you were traveling home. It's the princess..."

"What? What has happened to Vicky?"

"Since when have you become so informal with Her Royal Highness?" the duchess asked sharply.

"Never mind that, what has happened to her?" Billy demanded.

"She has been kidnapped, apparently snatched from ... Billy? Where are going?" she called to his back as he ran from the room."

"Back to London!" he called from the hallway.

CHAPTER 14

Everyone stood as Queen Victoria entered, followed by her lady-in-waiting, the Duchess of Sutherland, her mother, the Duchess of Kent, and the ever-present servant, John Brown. All present were taken with how frail, nearly gaunt, the queen looked. It had been three days since her daughter had been kidnapped, and the experience was taking its toll.

The Privy Council had rarely met in recent years, only being convened when the marriages of the queen's Cambridge cousins required her formal consent to marry. In addition to the fifteen active members of the Privy Council, also reclaiming their seat once the Queen had hers was former Prime Minister Derby, Mr. Disraeli, the newly installed P.M., the Earl Russell, who also served as the leader of the House of Lords, the Home Secretary, Sir George Lewis, and Duke Nikolaus of Oldenburg.

"Pray gentlemen, is there progress?" was all the queen could bear to ask. Her voiced waivered even then.

Sir George answered, "Your Majesty, we are working closely with Scotland Yard. They continue to detain and aggressively question known republican activists and agitators, but thus far they have not turned up any clues to who the kidnapper or kidnappers might be."

Lord Russell added, "Your majesty, I have made it clear that all members of Parliament who consider themselves republicans are to cooperate to the fullest extent with all police instructions as well. Given the circumstances, there has been no resistance."

"And of this criminal's demands?" the queen asked.

"Ma'am, his demand to change the entire nature of our form of government is not something that could be done in short order, even if we were inclined to do so."

"What if I offered to abdicate?" Murmurs of discontent filled the room.

Disraeli, considered the resident constitutional scholar, answered, "Your Majesty, I would counsel against anything so extreme. For one, it would not meet the demands of changing the form of government. And secondly, under the current situation, a Regency would have to be formed, likely in the person of the Duke of Cambridge, and that action would in all likelihood be contested by the King of Hanover, creating more problems than we need now." The Duke and the King were the last two surviving male grandchildren of George III, with Hanover being the genealogically more senior, but being king of a foreign nation, not a first choice for a regency in Britain.

"Of course, you are right. Our Cousin Cambridge is not well suited to the role anyway." The queen was still not ready to forgive the duke for marrying without her consent some ten years previously, a marriage though not legally recognized, he continued to maintain with "Mrs. Fitzgeorge."

"If I might say, Ma'am," Lord Russell continued, "this idea of holding an entire government hostage is nothing short of terrorism, a term thus far applied to the actions of a state against her people, but now used in the reverse. As a nation, we cannot give in to it. If we did, anyone with a fool notion of how things should be run might take a crack at it. We must allow Scotland Yard more time to find the villain and rescue Her Royal Highness."

More murmurs, of agreement this time, came from around the room.

"But what if this beast grows tired of waiting for action?" Victoria implored.

Sir George picked up the thread again. "We propose publishing a letter on the front page of *The Times* to the kidnapper advising that it is beyond our ability to meet his demands in anything resembling a timely manner. Afterall, Parliament will not even be in session again until the New Year." Taking a notable breath, he continued. "With your permission, Ma'am, we would like to make him a counteroffer. If he releases the princess unharmed, and leaves the country, he will not be pursued."

This time the murmurs around the room were mixed. But the government's representatives present were all aware that while this offer would be made to the kidnapper, no one was prepared to allow him to leave the country, except perhaps to be sent to Hell.

"Do you think," the queen began, but faltered, "that...that..she is...still alive?" Victoria slumped in her chair. The Duchess of Sutherland was at her side like a shot, feeling her wrists, thankful for a pulse.

"Get the doctor!" she ordered. But it John Brown who stepped in, lifting the diminutive monarch in his muscular arms and carried her from the room, over the protestations of those present.

"Send the doctor to her chambers," he said to Sutherland, and carried her off.

***

Col. Everton-Smythe was not the least bit surprised when young Capt. St. Albans came barging into his office. He was surprised, however, at his appearance: civilian clothes, unshaved, looking like he had not slept a wink in three days.

"Colonel," St. Albans began, but Everton-Smyth held up his hand to cut him off.

"Yes, you may cut your furlough short. I am assigning you to the attachment that is aiding Scotland Yard in the search for the princess. You will report to Major Bowen, but only after you have bathed, shaved, and gotten a full night's sleep, so that you can walk *through* my door rather than *into* it. Understood, Captain?"

"Yes, sir!" St. Albans said smartly and carefully walked out the office, gingerly closing the door behind him.

For the first time in three days, Col. Everton-Smythe dared to smile.

***

Vicky was pretty sure this was her fourth day here. With no windows she could not be quite certain. Her only way to count the days was by the type of food she was brought and trying to gauge her internal clock. What she thought was the morning meal always included a bit of meat, whether it was sausage or bacon, and a bowl of some sort of porridge. The midmeal, which she assumed was luncheon, was the simple bread and cheese, and the evening meal typically had some variety of bean soup. Each meal was accompanied by a small pitcher of water, but no fork or knife, requiring her to have to do everything with her hands. She at least got a spoon with the soup.

Given she had nothing better to do, she slept much of the time in between. At least she had begun to see a little of her captor, and yes he was the same man from the garden. As she never saw anyone else, nor heard them, she began to believe he was a one-man operation. He came in three times a day, to bring each meal, the morning visit often before she woke. Apparently at that time he emptied out the chamber pot for she would find it emptied, if not cleaned when she woke.

She tried a few times to speak to him, but he completely ignored her. He only reacted to her presence at all if she made any move while he was in the room, and then only to potentially protect himself or prevent her for bolting out. Since there was no handle on this side of the door, he had to leave it ajar when he entered.

143

On this fourth day, yes she was sure now it was the fourth, he entered with her bread and cheese. *Oh this much be luncheon.*

"Has there been a response from the Palace? Will they pay your ransom?" she blurted out.

"You think this is all about money? Of course, you would!" he spat at her. He set the food on the table and walked out again.

He speaks! she thought sarcastically. *But if he is not holding her for ransom, then why? And what did he mean "of course I would" think it was about money?*

She nibbled at her bread and cheese like a mouse. She had been playing a game since day two, or was it day three? The more slowly she ate, the longer she would make the food stretch. And playing this game kept her from sleeping too much. But even so, she would eventually drift off again until the next meal.

When she was awake, her thoughts kept drifting to Billy. She knew she should be focused on Niko, but she just couldn't keep her thoughts there. Billy was all she could think about since that night at the ball, which now seemed an eternity ago, even though it was only a few days. When she slept, it was always Billy she saw proposing. Sometimes she dreamed she said yes to him, only to have Niko dragging her away. The more time away from them both, the more she realized she only really missed one.

***

"Now, what am I gonna do with ya?" John Stockley asked the other side of the thick door he had just exited.

Lying before him was today's *Times* with the government's ultimatum splashed across the front page. "They won't give in, not even for their precious princess. Boot-lickers, the whole lot of 'em! An' what kind a fool do they take me for? Like they would let me outta the country. We're on a bleedin' island, ain't we? How am I suppose ta leave without them knowin' it? Won't pursue...sure they won't...won't need to...they'll snatch me right there at the coast."

He poured himself another whiskey in his single tin cup. It was the same one he drank what passed for his morning coffee out of. The outer room in which he sat was not much more furnished than the one where the princess sat.

This had once been a butcher shop owned by his step-father. A vile old man if ever there was one. But living with a butcher meant they never starved. The daily beatings were almost worth it for that alone. John didn't remember his actual father. According to his mum, he lost his way coming home from the pub one night and never did turn up. She had him declared dead after she took up with Sam the butcher. That was easier than a woman trying to get a divorce. Besides, Sam was old and decrepit enough that she'd really be a widow soon enough.

After the old coot croaked, his mum tried to carry on alone, but it was just too much for her. John tried to help, but the stench of the slaughtered animals was more than he could take, so the shop eventually closed. It was still in his mother's name, but she moved across the river to Bermondsey. Married a nice gent there and put the squalor of Whitechapel behind her. Now John has found another use for it, storing abducted princesses.

The more he drank, the more sinister the thoughts running through his mind got. Remembering back to his days slaughtering pigs into sausage, he came to the realization that a princess' neck is a lot thinner than a pig's. Easier to cut through.

CHAPTER 15

At Buckingham Palace, Dr. John Snow exited the queen's chamber. Several anxious people, including her ladies in waiting, Niko, John Brown, and the Prime minister were all waiting in her parlor, some of them having been there all night, others coming and going as their work permitted.

"Her Majesty has regained consciousness." the doctor informed those assembled, who collectively sighed in relief. "But the strain of the past few days is taking its toll. I have advised her to remain in bed and relax. As news of her daughter becomes available it can be brought to her. But I cannot stress enough the need for rest. Lady Sutherland, she would like you to attend her now." She curtsied and went into the queen's room, followed by her other ladies, except for Louie, who was still technically assigned to Vicky.

"Thank you, Doctor," the Prime Minister said. "You Highness," he addressed Niko, "you have been here nonstop all night. Please have the staff prepare a room for you, get some sleep. Once you are rested, perhaps there will be more news. Lady Louisa, could you please see to a room for the duke?"

"Of course, Prime Minister." Louie had been filling her days waiting on the queen as needed, not knowing what else to do with herself since Vicky's disappearance. Not having any other place to be, she was amongst those waiting for word on the queen's condition. Now she was thankful to have at least something to fill a few minutes of her time. Niko followed her out as the PM also made his exit to return to Westminster, leaving John Brown alone with the doctor.

"Mr. Brown," the doctor began. "I'm going to tell you what I dared not tell the PM, because you seem to be the only man within Her Majesty's intimate circle, even closer, it would seem, than her future son-in-law." The doctor halted a second, taking a deep breath.

"Out with it, man!" Brown ordered.

"I believe Her Majesty is with child," the doctor finally blurted out.

Brown stepped back half a step, his hand involuntarily going to his chest, his knee started to buckle. He caught himself and stood upright again.

"If I am correct, she is in a very early stage and likely has not realized it yet herself. Her concern for the princess will likely cause her to not notice anything amiss for the immediate time being, and I have not told her my suspicions. In her state, I am concerned about how it would affect her health. She is already feeling too much pressure."

"And what do ye expect me to do this knowledge?" Brown asked.

"As I said, you seem to be the only man in her intimate circle, so I'll be quite blunt. You are the prime suspect to have caused this situation. If I'm wrong, I apologize in advance, however, I feel you are in the best position to counsel the queen on how to proceed."

"It would seem to me the situation will proceed rather on its own." Brown retorted, ignoring the accusation.

"That's the more troublesome part of this development. I am sure you are aware the queen suffered a miscarriage in the immediate aftermath of Prince Albert's assassination. What was not made public at that time, and was only told to me by my predecessor, was that the miscarriage caused internal damage to Her Majesty and it would be very dangerous to her health to attempt to carry another child to term. This is the reason there was not much pressure from the government or from her own family for her to remarry and keep trying for a male heir."

"Will she survive this?" Brown asked, emotion choking the words.

"If she carries the child to term, it will be precarious. However, there are much safer means to remove the forming tissue with the use of certain medications. These means must be applied in the next few weeks to be effective. The longer the wait, the more discomfort it will cause Her Majesty."

Brown thought for several minutes before responding. He sat down as the gravity of the situation struck him fully. "The Queen's only close heir is her girl, the missing princess," he said finally and very quietly. "After that, the whole bundle goes to some

German bloke. If we don't get her back, this child she carries could be the next king or queen."

"If the child were to survive, and the odds are not in its favor. And let's not forget one important part to that: the Queen is not married, therefore the child would not have succession rights anyway."

"That part is easily remedied, just needs a vicar."

"And furthermore," the doctor continued, "even if, God willing, the princess is returned to us, a boy born to Her Majesty would immediately take precedence in the succession, upsetting nearly twenty years of expectation of a future Queen Victoria II.

"Let's leave that concern in God's hands. If it His will, then we must make do," Brown responded.

"I cannot stress enough the danger the queen will put herself in if she does not terminate this pregnancy. I guess my real question to you is, will you do your duty as the father?"

"I will do as I always have, whatever the Queen commands."

***

What a wretched place this is! Billy thought for not the first time today. As his horse plodded through the filth and mud that made up the so-called streets of London's East End. Whitechapel, the heart of the East End, had been the dung hole of London since Roman times. Being the first or last fringe of the metropolitan area, depending on if you were coming or going, and far removed from the more proper neighborhoods, it became the home of the lesser trades and their tradesmen, or tradeswomen in the case of the whorehouses. Blacksmiths, tanners, slaughterhouses all flourished here, and if one breathed into too deeply, they'd get a good whiff of the lot of them.

He tried to put the epitome of despair out of his mind and focus on his mission: finding Vicky. Scotland Yard had provided Major Bowen with a list of known republican agitators. Billy was assigned to locate five of them last known to live in the East End. The first three on the list all had good alibis for the day Vicky was taken, the fourth, John Stockley, was not home, and no one else appeared to live there. He now approached the home of number five, Ian MacKenneth.

His knock brought a middle-aged rosy cheeked lady to the door. "Yes?"

"Is this home of Ian MacKenneth?" Billy asked in a professional manner.

"Well, it used to be. It's in my name, now," the lady answered.

"Can you tell me where I can MacKenneth?"

"What is all of this about? I can't think of any reason the military would have with Old Mac."

"My unit is assisting with a police inquiry."

"Now, *that* sounds more like Old Mac. Well, whatever he's done, you're too late to do anything about it."

"How so?"

"If you want to find Ian MacKenneth, you'll have to go look in the churchyard. I'm afraid he's beyond answering any of your questions now, though."

"You mean he's dead?" Billy asked.

"And buried these past three months," the lady answered.

"Well, that absolves him of the crime we're investigating, it only happened within the last week."

"Oh my," he lady said, suddenly putting her hand to her heart. "You're looking for the princess."

"What makes you think that?" Billy asked.

"Would the military be helping the police on anything less? And it is the *only* crime that has happened in the past week worth mentioning, ain't it?"

"I don't suppose you would know anything about it, now would you, Ma'am?"

"Oh, I dare say not! I might not be so keen on the Lord-n-Lady crowd, but it's absolutely beastly to steal a child from her mum. I wouldn't wish that on anyone, not even Ole Vic herself."

"I see. By the way, do you happen to know a man named John Stockley? He is on my list of people to question, but I have not been able to find him."

"I only know of him. If there is a protest anywhere, he is likely in the middle of it. He always looks to be an angry man. Must've gotten it from his dad, his mum was the nicest thing. Sam, though, he was a crusty one, that guy."

"You knew her?"

"O yes, she had a butcher shop three streets over. It's closed down now. I guess Stockley was too busy raising Hell to worry about cutting meat."

"Do you know where I could find his mother?"

"I imagine she'd be getting on in years at this point, if she's even still alive. After the butcher died, she married again to a much nicer gent, then went to live with him somewhere across the river. I have no idea where."

"I see. Well, thank you for the nice chat," Billy said as he returned to horse.

"I really do hope you find her, the princess, I mean," Mrs. MacKenneth called to him.

Now what? Billy thought as he looked down at his list. He decided to go back to Stockley's house one more time. Maybe he was home now.

***

"Ah, the soup course. It must be evening time," Vicky quipped as her captor set her broth on the table. As usual, he said nothing, although she noticed he set the bowl down rather clumsily, slopping some soup on the table.

Rather than leaving, this time he lingered in the doorway. She began sipping her soup self-consciously as he stared. "Yes?" she finally asked.

"I'm just tryin' ta figure what ta do with ya. They refused my ransom demand," the way his words were slurring, Vicky suspected he had been drinking.

"I thought you said this was not about money," she pointed out.

"There's other types of ransom," he said. "See, I'm doing all of this for England. This could be a great country, everybody gettin' paid decent, have nice houses, three meals a day. But it can't happen as long as those fat hogs in Westminster keep the cream on top." He took another swig from his cup which was sitting just outside the door. Vicky could smell even from where she sat it was whiskey.

"I don't understand," she said.

153

"No, you wouldn't, would you? You've never hafta worry 'bout money. Hell, you never even hafta think about it, do ya? Well, let me tell ya, I hafta worry 'bout it ev'ryday. But I wouldn't if'ta wealth were spread around a bit. No royals, no nobles, jus' people."

"Oh, so this is a Marxist exercise, then?" In her efforts to learn more about the world, she read everything she could get her hands on that she felt would give her knowledge enough to be an effective queen. This included the works of Voltaire, Machiavelli, Locke, and even Karl Marx.

"I don't know what that is, but I'm just helping the natural fall of monarchy. Someone had to light the match in France, and all those revolutions about ten years ago. Now it's England's turn. But your mum ain't going down without a fight. An' you could learn a lesson here 'bout what you're worth to her. Given a choice between you and her crown, guess which she picked. I'll give ya a hint, you're still sittin' here."

"Well, that was a pretty bold gamble," Vicky pointed out. "Even if Mama abdicated, there would still be a Crown, except then it would sit on a foreign head, the King of Hanover's. At least with me, it stays right here in Britain where it belongs."

"Abdicate? Hell, girlie, I was going for ta whole shootin' match. I told Westminster to end the monarchy."

"That *was* bold." After a moment's thought, she pointed out, "Even if the government were so inclined, and I suspect there might have been one or two who would have agreed with you, that is not something that could be done in just these past few days. Parliament simply doesn't move that quickly, and in fact, they won't even be in session again until after the New Year."

"None of that mattered, they said 'No' flat out. So now I'm back ta what do I do about you." He was swaying slightly and glaring at her through glassy eyes.

"It would seem to me your gamble failed. And if you kill me, you only make matters worse for yourself and for the country you claim to love so much. The only logical course of action is to let me go!" Having listened to her captor's sniveling she realized he was a weak man and if she were going to get out of this, she had to take the bull by the horns and be firm with him.

"I can't very well let ya just walk on out of here." He now moved closer to the table and put his hands on it to steady himself.

"Of course you can. I have no idea who you are; I can't really identify you that well. If you quickly left London, you could easily hide in another part of the country. They'd probably never find you. I'll even be sporting about it and give you a fifteen minute head start. Just go on, leave the door open, and I'll wait fifteen minutes before I go outside and start figuring out how to get home from here."

"Girlie, you're a long way from home. Why, we could make our own little home right here." He snatched her wrist, surprising her at fast he could move in his state. In a moment, he was around the table. "I saw in ta paper you're engaged to some Russian bloke."

As she struggled to free herself from his grasp, he pulled her to him and spun her so she was now pressed up against him, his vice-like grip on her wrist never letting up.

155

"It'd be a shame ta spoil a good English girl like yurself on some Hun's filthy prick." With his free hand, he started unfastening his trousers. "You deserve some 100% English Oak."

Vicky knew where his hands were headed and she fought to stop them. She scoured the room for an escape, but it was so bare. In frustration she screamed, not knowing what else to do. In trying to wiggle out of his grasp, she bumped the table, making what was left of her soup slosh onto it. She grabbed for the bowl with her free hand and spun as much and as hard she could, shoving the remaining contents of the bowl into her attacker's face.

He stumbled slightly, loosening his grip on her wrist. She quicky got out of his embrace, spinning to face him. She saw he managed to free himself from his trousers and they had fallen to his knees, his swollen penis pointing at her menacingly. He teetered with his legs partially bound as they were, so she tried to run around him to get to the door. He tried to grab her again, but she was too fast; he only got a grip on the material from her dress.

But she was snagged and unable to get away and was now facing his back. With both hands, she pushed him as hard as she could, trying to free her dress from his clutches. His legs got tangled in their garments and he lurched forward. With one more great heave, Vicky heard the material tear away from his fingers, and she bolted for the door.

She turned reflexively when she heard him scream in pain, but only looked back long enough to see he had landed on the stove, his naked man flesh pressed against the heated cast iron. Then she ran out the door, through the ante chamber and out into the street.

CHAPTER 16

Billy stood before the door he had knocked on before. He listened intently. No sounds from within gave away any sheltering fugitives. But could John Stockley be hiding inside? With Vicky's life in the balance he finally decided he could not risk just walking away. From what he learned about Stockley, this sounded like the best lead yet to finding the missing princess.

He tried the doorknob, it was solidly locked, but the wood around it was old and weathered. With a couple of tries with both his shoulder and his boot, he managed to break the door in. It was a small house with a single-story. The front room was clearly also the main room of the house. A small kitchen was in the back corner with a hallway running alongside that likely went to the bedrooms.

Able to look around the entire living room, dining area, and kitchen without taking a step, he ascertained they were empty and moved toward the bedrooms. The hallway revealed a small water closet and two bedrooms. The first bedroom was clearly where Stockley slept. The bed was unmade and a small chest of drawers held his few clothes. The second bedroom, however, was a different tale.

Though devoid of life, the room was by no means empty. It had been converted into a workshop. On the worktable were various shells and other parts to what Billy recognized as grenades. On the wall were tacked newspaper articles, mostly about the Queen and the Princess Royal. Most notably, the Court Circular, had been torn from several days' worth of papers and were tacked in date order. He was tracking their movements. The most recent was the day of the kidnapping.

Billy now knew this was his man. If he hadn't been, the Court Circular of the past several days would also be there. The partially assembled explosives also told Billy this man meant to end the royal family and do so violently. But where was he now, and where did he have Vicky?

He considered removing the small amount of TNT he found, but then thought better of it. It would be best if Stockley didn't know anyone had been there. Oh, but the door. There was no way to hide that damage. Then all that was left was to try to make it as unnoticeable as possible and then hunker down somewhere close by and watch for Stockley to return. He planned to nab him at the door, hopefully before he noticed it had been broken into.

Returning outside, he closed the door and tried to place the broken lock in as much as a normal-looking position as possible. Once satisfied it would pass until someone got truly close to it, he next had to find a place to stash his horse. The closest police office was only two streets over, he could leave her there. He was just hoisting himself back into the saddle when he heard the scream. It was unmistakably a woman and it came from the opposite direction as the police station. He raced to find its origin.

***

Once Vicky was out in the street, she tried to get her bearings. Typical for a November evening in London, the sky was uniformly dark gray, the heavy clouds masking the location of the moon or the stars which might give her a sense of direction. The lack of moonlight also made the street darker and scarier than it would have been in the daylight.

She could tell right off it was an underprivileged area. It looked like nothing of the portion of London she was familiar with. These streets were rather narrow, and the buildings, a mixture of wood and brick, were all in need of refreshing. Some could get by with a new coat of paint, but many had structural defects that had not been addressed. And the streetlights were further apart than in the Kensington area, and seemed to be less bright as well. Looking closely at the nearest one, she could tell this was partly due the globes not being cleaned regularly, if ever.

The sounds of her captor's pain increased, meaning he was up and trying to pursue her. She ran to the corner of an alley across the street where she could hide in the shadows. Too late she realized she left footprints in the mud. Then she saw him in the doorway, now holding something in his hand. She could just make out that it was a knife. He wasn't wearing his trousers, only a leather apron, which he seemed to be trying to hold away from his body as best as he could. Perhaps the pain from his burns were too much for trousers. He looked both left and right deciding which way to go, before he saw the footprints in the mud leading to the alleyway.

She looked around her quickly. Her eyes had now adjusted to the low light and she saw she was standing next to a wagon wheel with a few broken spokes lying on the ground. She grabbed one of the spokes to use as a weapon if she needed to and sunk further into the alley trying to hide among the other rubbish that had been left there.

She held her breath as she waited for her kidnapper to appear at the mouth of the alley. But instead she heard a loud and authoritative voice. And amazingly, it was a familiar voice. "You there, stop!" Was that horse hooves she heard?

Vicky inched toward the end of the alley and looked around the corner with just one eye. She could not believe what she was seeing. But it was true. There was Billy on a horse addressing her kidnapper. The half-naked thug had stopped advancing toward the alley when challenged by someone in uniform.

Billy started dismounting. Now Vicky could see the glint of the knife in her attacker's hand. He was turned slightly to hide it from Billy. She stepped out of the alley.

"He has a knife!" she screamed.

With one foot still in the stirrup, Billy lunged himself backwards away from his mount which added a little distance between him and the man he stopped. Landing on the ground at the same time he pulled his sword, he was able to get the length of it up just in time for the knife-wielding maniac to run right into the tip.

The attacker's momentum kept him moving forward far enough for the sword to penetrate his heart. Afterwards, he slumped to the ground, dead.

Vicky ran to Billy from her alley hiding place, throwing her arms around him. "You came for me!"

"Of course, I did. It was my duty," Billy said trying to sound detached, almost succeeding. "Are you injured?"

"No, I'm fine," Vicky answered.

Not quite knowing how to ask what he knew he must, he came up with, "Dare I ask why he is not wearing trousers?"

"He attacked me, but I was able to fight him off. In the process, he landed on the stove."

Billy used the toe of boot to roll his attacker over, causing the apron to flip up. Before he could focus on the face, he grimaced when saw the damage done by the hot iron of the stove. "I'd say killing this man was a mercy." He removed a blanket from his horse and draped it over the body for decency's sake, taking a good look at the face before he did. "Looks like Stockley's description. Did he tell you his name?"

"No, he said precious little to me until today. Then he got rather chatty with the help of some whiskey. He said this was all an attempt to get rid of the monarchy."

"That was clear from his demands."

By this time, a few onlookers had come out of the buildings along the street to see what was happening. After Vicky pointed out which building had been her prison, he asked in loud question, "Do any of you know who lives in that building?" pointing to the one Vicky indicated.

"No one lives there, it used to be a butcher shop, but's been closed for years." One man piped up. "Who are you?"

"I'm a soldier of the Home Guard. This man was chasing this lady with a knife. His death was in defense of myself and her. You have nothing to fear from me." Billy, still holding his sword, put it back in its scabbard. "Who here knows what John Stockley looks like?"

"I'd know his ugly mug anywhere," said one woman. From her attire, Billy was pretty sure she was a prostitute.

"Can you please tell me if this man is Stockley?"

She hesitantly came forward, not knowing what to expect when he drew the blanket back.

Billy was careful only to expose his face, not wanted to offend the lady with the dead man's ugly burns, not to mention the parts where they were located.

"Yeah, that's him. You done society a good turn killin' that one, ya did."

"Thank you, Ma'am," Billy said politely and covered the cadaver back up. He saw a lad, who looked to be about fourteen or so, slinking closer to the body trying to get a look. "You boy, you want to earn a shilling?"

"Wha' for?" he asked.

Billy reached in his pouch and fetched out a coin. Tossing it to the boy, he said, "Go get a police officer and bring him here. Tell him what's happened."

The boy ran off and Billy pulled off his cloak and wrapped it around Vicky's shoulders and pulled the hood up over her head. Then he whispered to her, "until we get you out of here, let's keep who are our little secret." She nodded.

Soon, the boy returned with the local bobby in tow. Billy took him aside and quietly told him the situation. The officer agreed to take care of the body. Then Billy helped Vicky onto his horse, where she sat sidesaddle as far forward as she could, so he could sit astride just behind her. In this position they could not ride very fast, but he kept them going as fast as he could safely.

"I'm so sorry!" Vicky blurted out once they were out of earshot from the crowd gathering at the scene they just left.

"You have nothing be sorry for. Stockley's the sorry one," Billy pointed out. "Now he's paid for his crime, so it's over."

"No, it was all my fault. If I had not been so stupid at the ball, you would not have left, and he never would have gotten so close to me to start with."

"Actually, you might have saved *my* life," Billy pointed out. That blighter killed the man who was supposed to be your guard. If I had not left, that could have been me.

"But I was wrong. You shouldn't have left before we talked. But then, I should have gone to you right away, but was too ashamed. I knew almost immediately I was wrong. I don't know what happened. Niko had me there in the middle of the whole crowd with everyone looking on, expecting me to say 'yes' to him, I did it without thinking. But I don't want to marry Niko. I want you!"

"I thought you weren't ready —"

"That was before. I have been locked up for a week now with nothing to do but think about what a mess I

165

made of this. I even promised God I'd straighten this out if only He spared me. Well, He sent you to me, so I guess he's going to hold me to it."

Billy had slowed the horse to a walk so they could hear each other. "What about all those people who you said they wouldn't let me marry you?"

"I'll tell them they have no choice. One thing that, that man —"

"Stockley?"

"Whatever his name is, er was, one thing he made me realize. I have more power than I thought. If anything were to happen to me, there would be a foreigner on the Throne. There's no way they will be deny me the husband I want. And I have rehearsed every argument I can think of for why it is better I marry an Englishman than a foreign prince."

"So then, is that a yes?"

"A yes to what?" she asked coyly.

"Princess Victoria Adelaide, will you marry me?"

"Yes, absolutely, unreservedly yes"

The couple enjoyed a long-awaited kiss before spurring the horse to get them back to Buckingham Palace as quickly as possible.

CHAPTER 17

On the way, Billy told Vicky her mother had taken ill and was being kept in bed. He said it appeared to be stress from the kidnapping and assured his fiancée that having her home would be just was the queen needed.

As soon as they got to the palace, there was immediate celebrations among the servants who met them. Before going to see her mother, Vicky insisted on Louie helping her to get cleaned up and dressed in something, anything, she had not been wearing for a week.

Meanwhile, Billy went to his barracks to report all that happened to Col. Everton-Smythe. Scotland Yard and the Home Office were contacted and soon, Billy found himself repeating the same facts over and over until everyone had the story straight.

Vicky was getting the same drilling from Louie, who wanted to know every detail. Finally satisfied that Vicky was none the worse for wear from her terrifying ordeal, she got her dressed in all clean clothes—with explicit instructions to burn what she had been wearing—and took her to her mother's bedchamber.

Sitting just outside, looking more like a guard than a simple servant, was John Brown. He welcomed Vicky and told her how much her safe return would mean to her mother. He oddly did not mention anything about her health.

Vicky left John and Louie both in the anteroom and went in to see her mother alone. Sitting in a chair next to the bed was the ever-faithful Duchess of Sutherland. She was working on her sewing in between bouts of tending to the queen. The two women hugged briefly, the Duchess in tears seeing the princess safe and sound, then she moved outside to leave mother and daughter alone.

"Mama?" Vicky whispered coarsely. The queen didn't stir.

"Mama?" she said a little louder.

"Vicky? Where are you, Baby?" Victoria was obviously stuck between consciousness and dreamland. "Why can't I find you?"

"But I am found, Mama. Billy found me. I'm right here. Just open your eyes and you'll see."

Queen Victoria's eyes fluttered slightly and then she saw her daughter. Bolting upright in bed, she screamed, "Vicky!"

The two hugged and cried, and Vicky patiently answered all the same questions Louie pelted her with, finally convincing her mother that she was alright and she was really back.

"Help me to the chair, Honey," the queen ordered.

"I thought you were supposed to stay in bed."

"Doctors!" she exclaimed. "If I let them have their way, I'd be petrified and half-way in the grave by now.

I'm fine, I'm fine. Seeing you makes everything else fine!"

Vicky helped her mother to the chair where Sutherland had been sitting, and then pulled a second chair over to sit next to her.

"Have you seen Duke Nicolas yet?" the queen asked.

"No, I came straight here."

"Well, he has been staying in the Palace since you disappeared. You must see him and let him know you are alright."

"But, Mama, I'm not alright, not as far as Niko goes," Vicky confessed.

"Oh?"

"I've had a lot of time to think this past week, nothing else to do but think, in fact. And now I know who it is I love ... and it's not Niko. I want to marry Billy."

"Does he also still want this?"

"Yes."

"I see," her mother fell silent for a few seconds, closing her eyes and thinking. Finally, she opened them again. "There will be push back from the government. I know the foreign minister was already talking to the Russians about various trade agreements. They were hoping to turn our former enemies in to future military allies, as well."

"They can still do all of that, if it what is best for both countries. And if it not, then our marriage would not have helped that situation any."

"They seem to think it would have been a good alliance, and your marriage to Tsar's cousin would help it along."

"But is that what my marriage is to be, a business deal between nations?"

"Many a royal marriage has been just that," the queen countered, but saw the horrified look on her daughter's face. "Don't worry, dear. I was allowed to marry for love, so will you be. But it will be a hard sell. No heir-apparent or sovereign has married a commoner since Henry VIII, and well, that didn't go so good."

"No, he was very good at getting married. His problem was staying married," Vicky pointed out. Both women laughed at that. "Besides, Billy is not completely a commoner. He is a direct male-line descendant of Charles II, after all."

"*And* an actress, not his wife. But you have a point. He does have some royal blood. Very well, you have my blessing, but don't breathe a word of it until you clear the air with Nicolas."

Vicky thanked her mother, and spent a little more time just being mother and daughter, and happy to be together again. When the queen began to tire again, Vicky helped her back to bed, then left to go find Niko.

As it turned out, she didn't have to look hard. He was waiting for her in anteroom with Sutherland and Brown, who both went in to join the queen. Vicky thought it odd that John brown would go in as well, but Sutherland acted as nothing was out of the ordinary. She made a point to ask Louie about it later.

"Thank God! You're alright!" Niko exclaimed. He ran up and hugged Vicky, apparently not noticing she tensed in his arms.

"Yes Niko, I wasn't hurt, and the man who took me was killed. It's all over, now. I'm looking forward to putting it all behind me."

"I understand. We have so much to look forward to, perhaps focusing on that would be for the best."

"Niko, I have to talk to you about that, too." Vicky had no idea how to say what came next. She surprised herself she got that much out. She felt her way along, "while I was held in that place I had nothing to do there but think." She was really getting tired of telling everyone that.

"Oh, I suppose you have the wedding all planned out already?"

"No, that's not what I meant—"

"Well, I hope you left at least the honeymoon to me. Since we are getting married in June, I thought it would be incredibly romantic to go to St. Petersburg by ship. Maybe your mother could loan us that yacht they gave her that she never uses. You can meet all of my relatives in Russia. Then you'll know why I prefer to live—"

"Stop, Niko," Vicky finally interrupted him. "You did this the night of the ball, too. You went on with your plans and took me by surprise, so I didn't know what I was doing. And you were like that in Brussels."

"What do you mean?"

"I mean, I'm going to have *my* say, now. When you proposed, you did it in front of all the royals of Europe. Everyone assumed I would say yes, so it felt I had no choice. I said yes. But I do have a choice, Niko." She let out a deep breath and continued, "you are probably the most exciting person I have ever met. You are bold, brazen, an enormous flirt, and unafraid of anything."

"Thank you, I think."

"But none of that changes one small impediment to us getting married."

"What? If it is religion, I'll join the Anglican church. My mother is a Protestant, so I am already familiar with it."

"No, Niko, the problem is not religion," she put her fingers on his mouth to prevent him from going down another path. "The problem is, I don't love you. I'm so sorry. Before the ball, I kept telling myself I could force myself to love you—and your good looks did make that a little easier—but after a week of nothing to do but dwell on it, I realized that was not enough. I can't marry a man I don't love."

"But how do you know?"

"How do I know what?"

"That you don't love me? How much experience with love do you have to know the difference? Besides, I don't know any royals who truly love their spouses. All the princes I know have their wives, and then have the women whom they truly care for also."

"And is that what you expected?" Vicky's guilt at dumping her fiancé quickly turned to anger. "That I would tolerate you having mistresses on the side?"

"But...but...that's how it's done," Niko stammered.

"That might be how you do it in the frozen wasteland of Russia, but that is not what we do here!"

"Have you read a history of your own family?" Niko asked pointedly. "Lots more mistresses than there were wives."

"Your business here is done, Duke Nicolas, you may withdraw," Vicky stated flatly, her words edged with more ice than a St. Petersburg window ledge.

172

Niko could do nothing but bow deeply and turn to go. As he started to leave he said over his shoulder, "if you find this 'love' you seek, please write and let me know how you did it." Then he was gone.

CHAPTER 18
December 23, 1858

Vicky was happy to see her mother up and back at her duties by Christmastime. The queen had made the decision, at the suggestion of her doctors, to remain at Buckingham Palace this year for the holidays, so she busied herself with catching up on her boxes from the government.

Vicky was also especially thrilled to be attending her first Privy Council meeting. Despite having only turned seventeen the previous month, the queen reasoned her daughter had been through enough and was mature enough to handle the responsibility of sitting on the Privy Council. Besides, she was about to become a married woman. If she was old enough to do that, then she was capable of doing this.

No one on the council but Vicky and her mother knew for sure the reason for the meeting. However, several might have suspected. This would be where it was publicly announced for the first time that she was to marry Billy. The various members then could either except the news gracefully or choose to fight it. Vicky knew Billy had been working quietly behind the scenes to reduce opposition from his fellow Lords. They would soon know if he was successful.

Vicky and all of the men rose as Queen Victoria entered, attended by the ever-faithful Duchess of Sutherland, and oddly by John Brown. But Vicky knew she should not have been surprised. The Scotsman had been at her mother's side nearly every waking moment since she had returned from her ordeal. She assumed it was because the queen was still not at full strength yet and she relied on Smith's powerful frame to support her when necessary. And as he was her personal bodyguard, it probably gave her a sense of security that had been all but shattered in the past month.

Vicky also noticed her mother was dressed rather oddly. Her dress was pulled out at the waist and hung rather loose and fluid. Then she realized her mother was still not wearing a corset. When she first left her sickbed, she said it was on her doctor's orders to avoid pressure on her abdominal area until she had fully recovered. The difference in the way the queen's bosom rested inside her dress made it obvious, at least to her. She doubted any man in the room would have noticed. And if they did, they wouldn't dare mention it.

Settling herself in her throne-like chair at the head of the table, she began. "Gentlemen, pray be seated. I know you are anxious to return to your families at this festive time of year so I will not detain your for long. I have two items."

Vicky looked at her mother. *What could the second item be?*

"In accordance with the Royal Marriages Act of 1772, We hereby give Our consent in open council to the marriage of Our beloved daughter, Her Royal

Highness the Princess Royal, to His Grace the Duke of Saint Albans."

There were a few murmurs around the table, but no one spoke out in objection.

Her Majesty raised her hand to simmer them down. "The full details of the wedding will come about in due course, but I would recommend that you all keep June 5th next open in your schedules." With this she smiled at her daughter before returning to the matters at hand.

"Now, We are obligated to inform you that tomorrow, December the 24th, We shall be married in a private ceremony to Mr. John Brown."

For a moment, the room was so quiet a pin could have been dropped with deafening percussion, but only for a moment. Suddenly, everyone was talking at once. "Tomorrow?" "You can't!" "He's a commoner!" "This will end the monarchy!" and so on.

Victoria calmly twisted one of her larger, gaudier rings on her finger, and proceeded to use it as a gavel, slamming her hand on the table several times to silence the room. She proceeded in her usual calm quiet voice, "Yes, tomorrow, at 10 o'clock in the morning. Yes, I can. I am under no legal obligation to seek any permission to marry, only to advise that it is happening. He is no longer a commoner; before entering this meeting I signed the Patent granting John Brown the style, title, and dignity of His Grace the Duke of Edinburgh, Earl of Windsor, and Baron Osborne, to be gazetted and take effect tomorrow as we are pronounced man and wife. I offered him the rank of Prince, but he declined that dignity. Furthermore, also effective tomorrow, he shall be a member of this Privy

177

Council. And finally, the monarchy *will* continue. I believe Our subjects would wish for Us to be happy, and We know from previous experience that there is no happier state than that of matrimony with a loving and supportive companion. Gentlemen, this meeting is adjourned."

Everyone rose as the queen did. Despite nearly every member of Council wishing to object to this sudden bombshell, when the Sovereign says a meeting is done, it is done. They had no choice but to rise and bow as she exited. This, of course, did not mean they would not continue to discuss this development among themselves once she was out of earshot.

Victoria turned, was joined alongside by the soon-to-be Duke of Edinburgh, and left the room without another word, but with Sutherland and Vicky in tow. The men of her government were left to stare at each other. Not a one of them approved of this, but at the same time, they could do absolutely nothing about it.

***

The royal party walked in formal procession all the way to the queen's office. There, Sutherland was excused and Victoria, John, and Vicky went into the office alone.

The queen could tell Vicky was about to start an interrogation so she raised her had to stop her daughter before she even started. "Now, I doubt any of those stuffed shirts will give a second thought to the appropriateness of your pending nuptials with young Saint Albans." She winked at her daughter before sitting somewhat gingerly behind her desk. As she did so, she seemed to deflate as if it had taken all of her will to get through that meeting and the walk back.

"I am sorry to have blind-sided you with this, darling child," Victoria finally said. "But much has happened that you are not yet aware of, until now. In his time here, I have come to rely on John for so many things. I have more ministers than I can name to help me with affairs of state, but no one to attend me as a person, as a woman, since you precious father's death so long ago. John has filled that void.

"Mama, of course I am happy that you have found love again, but marriage? That was very sudden."

"I know child, but it was necessary. I knew I could not give the government a chance to object to my remarriage. God knows if they had that opportunity, they would take advantage of it. So, we decided to spring it on them without time for them to do anything about it. And doing it at the same Council meeting as announcing your engagement was John's idea. It gave them something to focus on rather than trying to interfere with your happiness."

"Well, Mr. Brown...I mean, John...I guess I am thankful for that."

"Your mother and I only want you to be happy. And by marrying your mum, I hope to show them all that a consort doesn't have to be some foreign prince. Perhaps then it will be a little easier for your feller."

"Now Vicky, there is a little more to the story, and I have already decided not to make this publicly known for several more months," she paused a second to take a breath, as if she was fortifying herself to say the rest. "But I am expecting another child."

"What... how... when...?" Vicky stammered. Then everything fell into place for her. She understood why her mother had been so ill, and why the marriage was happening so suddenly. Even why she still was not wearing a corset. All she could think to say was "oh, Mother!"

"My doctor tells me to expect the baby in July."

"Tell her the rest," John prompted.

"What are you not telling me?" Vicky demanded.

"My doctor, a man who make the most stable person into a hypochondriac, is overly concerned about my condition. He has been insisting I be far less active than I was when I carried you. I am following his orders...mostly, but John is worrying enough for the both of us." She gave her fiancé a mock-cross look. "He tends to forget that I have done this before, he hasn't. I admit I'm get tired easier this time, but I am not the spring chicken I was when you were born. But I'm afraid I am going to have to rely on you to carry out the public functions until the baby arrives."

"Of course, I will," Vicky assured her. "I'm going to be a sister?" Vicky was still in a state of disbelief. "I'm going to have a little brother or sister!" The something occurred to her. "Oh, my," she said with a deflated look.

"Yes, Sweetheart. If the baby is a boy, he will automatically become my heir. I am sorry about that, but it is the law. I know you have been groomed to take over some day, but if you do have a brother, I hope you will do everything to support him."

"Of course, I will." After a few more seconds contemplation, she added, "God Save the Duke of Cornwall!"

The wedding the following day went off without a hitch. It was a very small affair in the Chapel Royal, adjacent to St. James' Palace, less than a half-mile down the Mall from Buckingham Palace. The only attendees besides the bride, groom, and the Bishop of London were Vicky, who served as Maid of Honor, the Duchess of Sutherland, the Duchess of Kent, Billy, who stood in for Best Man since none of John's male relatives were close enough to attend, and John's sister, Caroline, who served at the neighboring Marlborough House.

Because there had been no public announcement of the wedding prior to it happening, there were no crowds to cheer the newlyweds, just the occasional curious passerby that might have happened to be on the street that day. Surely anyone who did see the short procession back to Buckingham would have been surprised to see the queen with a man sitting next to her in her carriage.

As could be expected the Christmas Eve evening editions of the papers were covered with the sensational headlines, QUEEN REMARRIES! with the less loyal rags running QUEEN MARRIES HER SERVANT! But never one to read the papers, the queen remained blissfully unaware.

CHAPTER 19
June 1859

For about two weeks, the story was on everyone's lips, but it did finally settle into the realm of "old news," as the nation started buzzing with the next wedding on the agenda, the upcoming nuptials of Vicky and Billy, or the "Princess and her Duke" as the media dubbed them. The public turned it into a fairytale wedding to rival Cinderella.

By the time the day arrived, Vicky was pretty sure she had met every one of her mother's subjects personally. Through the spring, she and Billy traveled the countryside, dedicating schools, hospitals, decorating military veterans, etc. on behalf of the queen. They would say Her Majesty was a bit too indisposed for travel, without mentioning the fact she was getting larger and larger with child.

It was only when the procession arrived at Westminster Abbey for the wedding that the cause of the queen's indisposition was apparent to all. She was now eight months pregnant and there was no hiding it. While the palace had put out a statement that the queen was expecting a few days before the wedding, they were very vague about the due date. Victoria had hoped to be able to claim premature labor when the time finally came to obscure the fact she had gotten the pregnancy and the marriage in backwards order.

The weather behaved beautifully for the wedding with plenty of sunshine and just a few fluffy white clouds lazily floating by to provide the spectators with welcome bouts of shade. Vicky was dressed in layered shades of off-white, complete with the traditional gifts of something old (the traditional coronet of a princess, first made for Princess Anne, daughter of George II), something new (an exquisite string of pearls she received as a wedding present from her grandmother), something borrowed (a set of her mother's pearl earrings that went perfectly with the necklace) and something blue (the sash that went with her Order of the Garter, which she received only the day before).

Billy also looked quite resplendent in his formal uniform as the newly-appointed Colonel-in-Chief of the Coldstream Guard. As he stood at the alter awaiting his bride he looked out over the guests and dreaded the idea he would have to get to know all of them and be able to recognize them on sight. Because Vicky was still technically the Heiress to the Throne, this was a full state ceremony and royals from all over Europe, as well as delegations from across the Empire were in attendance. And yet, because there was still a chance she would not be the next queen, the decision was made to not offer Billy the title of Prince at this time.

One person he did recognize was the Tsar of Russia, whom he was happy to see. He had feared they might send Duke Nicolas as a representative. But, as Vicky assured him, Niko had fallen out of favor ever since eloping with his mother's lady-in-waiting. Also present was one of Vicky's closest continental friends, Prince Fritz of Prussia. The two of them were determined to keep relations between their kingdoms happy and peaceful despite the machinations of Bismarck and Fritz's father.

When Queen Victoria made her entrance, the wave of murmuring that went through the church was almost palpable, the papers had been full of the news that she was pregnant again with a late-in-life baby but failed to mention how far along she was. The question was really she That close to delivery, or did she just gain a lot of weight with this child? Though she would soon be coming up on her Silver Jubilee, nearly everyone had to be reminded she was still only a woman of forty. No small part of the whispers in Westminster Abbey that day were also about the Duke of Edinburgh, the servant who was now a royal consort.

The royal entourage was rather impressive as they were rarely all together in one place at the same time. The queen was followed by her mother, sister, and nephew, the Duchess of Kent, Princess of Hohenlohe, and Prince of Leiningen, respectively, and then her Hanoverian cousins, the King and Queen of Hanover, the Duke of Cambridge, escorting his widowed mother, and his married sisters the Grand Duchess of Mecklenburg and the Duchess of Teck. Representing the Saxe-Coburgs were the Dowager Duchess, Vicky's step-grandmother, and the current Duchess, wife of Vicky's Uncle Ernie. Ernie himself had been selected to walk Vicky down the aisle in place of her missing father, his brother.

As the bridal processional started, Billy smiled at his sisters, both chosen to be bride's maids. They were followed by Louie, who was Maid of Honor. The gentlemen selected to be groomsmen were picked to accentuate Billy's own connection to royalty. They were the Dukes of Buccleuch, Grafton, and Richmond, the other direct male-line descendants of King Charles II, each one descended from a different mistress. When the bride finally entered there was a collective sigh as her gown gave the impression of a goddess shrouded by clouds.

The ceremony itself was rather simple, a far cry from the lengthy Catholic affair they had witnessed in Brussels just two years previously. When all was said and done, the couple and all of their royal guests returned to Buckingham for the wedding luncheon.

***

The luncheon was going along festively. There were toasts to the bride and groom, to the queen, even to her forthcoming baby. At the head table the queen was seated between her new son-in-law, Billy, and his new step-father, the Viscount of Falkland. Then during dessert, it happened.

Victoria clutched Billy's wrist in a death grip and drew in a gasp, audible even at the next table. All she was able to get out was, "the baby!" and collapsed against Billy. Before her full weight had time to settle against him, John was suddenly there, lifting his wife from the chair and carrying her off like a shot.

"Louie, get the doctor!" Vicky screamed over her shoulder as she followed on John's heels, Billy only one step behind her.

It was the Duchess of Teck, born Princess Mary of Cambridge, who took control of the banquet. Her generous proportions were often a hinderance in day-to-day life and earned her the smear in the nastier press as "Fat Mary," but when she needed to vocally settle a room, she definitely had a strong enough diaphragm and the deep baritone voice for it.

Meanwhile, John rushed the queen to her chambers, his muscular legs carrying them both with ease. Vicky, once clear of the banquet hall, threw etiquette to the wind, hoisted her skirts to her knees and ran to keep up. They had only gotten the queen out of her formal gown and onto the bed by the time Sutherland showed up and assisted. They got Victoria into bed, still unconscious. At first they thought her water had broken, but once they had her down to her petticoats, the amount of blood told something more dire was happening.

Louie arrived shortly with Dr. Snow and Mrs. Sutton, the midwife, in tow. As the doctor started tending to the queen, Mrs. Sutton shooed everyone else out of the room. The Duchess of Sutherland, a trained nurse, stayed to assist the doctor as necessary. John initially objected to leaving his wife's side and scoffed at the idea of Mrs. Sutton, throwing him out despite her being a sturdy woman.

"Your Grace, you are wearing a kilt. If I must physically remove you, I'll have no trouble finding a handle to grip," Sutton snarled at him. He left.

In the antechamber to the Queen's bedroom, they were joined by rest of her immediate family as well as the Prime Minister and the Leader of the Opposition, Lords Derby and Palmerston, respectively. They demanded to be let into the bedchamber as they were legally required to witness the birth of any child who might succeed the Throne. They were allowed in but ordered to remain in the far corner, out of the way.

After about thirty minutes, Derby and Palmerston came out again. It was Darby who addressed the Duke of Edinburgh, but loud enough for all to hear. "I regret to inform Your Grace that your child died in utero. The doctor is going to have to perform a Caesarian operation to remove the fetus. Her Majesty has not regained consciousness, and her very life is in danger. They are, of course, doing all they can for her. The next hour will tell the tale. May God save the Queen!"

"God save the Queen!" everyone repeated.

Vicky felt her knees weaken, and Billy helped her to a chair next to where her grandmother was already sitting.

"Don't vorry, sveetheart," the Duchess soothed. "Your mutter is a strong voman. If anyvun can survive tis, sie kans." Vicky hugged her. Somehow her broken English was just the comforting voice she needed right then. Her Aunt Feodora sat on the other side of her mother and held her hand, as Vicky turned to be held by her husband.

"I'm sorry, darling, this was not how either of us expected to spend our wedding night," Vicky said.

"Shhh. We have the rest of our lives for that," he soothed.

The next forty-five minutes ticked on but felt like forty-five hours. Finally, Dr. Snow emerged. He had removed his blood-soaked apron, but his sleeves told a tale of horror. Vicky stood as he approached, then he bowed to her.

"Your Majesty...," he began.

It hit Vicky like a ton of bricks. He could only say one thing after addressing her like that.

"...I'm terribly sorry to inform you the Queen passed away approximately fifteen minutes ago. The baby died while still inside her and poison from his decaying fetus had already infected Her Majesty's bloodstream by the time we could remove the fetus from her. There was nothing that could have been to preserve her life. If it is any comfort to Your Majesty, she never regained consciousness, so I do not believe she suffered any pain."

Vicky heard none of this and had to be reminded of it later by Billy. All she could do was cry into his chest as he held her close. They stood like that a few moments, and then remembering they were surrounded by several people, she wiped he eyes with a handkerchief produced by Louie. She looked first to her step-father. A mountain of a man, to see him standing stoically, but with tears running down face, was heart-wrenching.

After what seemed an appropriate pause, the P.M. stepped forward and in a quiet, sad voice, he intoned, "The Queen is dead, long live Queen Victoria the Second!"

"Long live Queen Victoria, God save the Queen!" the rest responded in somber tones.

It was decided to hold the funeral quickly as all of Europe was already there for the wedding. Therefore two days later, Vicky, still moving mostly as if in a trace, and with the help of Billy, found herself walking slowly behind the gun carriage carrying her mother's coffin. She realized as the procession moved slowly from Buckingham Palace to Westminster Abbey that she had until this moment never considered what must go into the planning of a royal funeral.

When she attended those of her grand aunts and uncles, the arrangements were all made outside of her knowledge and she merely had to show up. Even now, they brought very few details her, most had been arranged long ago by the Earl Marshal and other stewards of protocol. The only decision she had to make was whether to walk behind the coffin or ride with the other ladies of her family in a carriage.

She opted to walk. After everything that she and the country had gone through this past year, her people needed to see their new queen and see that she strong enough for the task ahead. She had already assured her Privy Council the day before she would be a different, more engaged, queen than her mother had been. It was there that her regnal name was formally acknowledged, and that she bestowed upon her husband the title, rank, and dignity of a Prince of the United Kingdom with the qualification His Royal Highness. She also established that henceforth they and their descendants would be House of Stewart, restoring to Billy his ancestral name denied his many time great-grandfather for simply being born outside a marriage.

Now they walked at a slow pace, she and Billy were followed by a row of her closest living relatives: the King of Hanover, who was now heir-presumptive, the Duke of Cambridge, the Crown Prince of Belgium—the king had been too frail to come to the wedding—and the Duke of Saxe-Coburg. Behind them, two carriages carried the late queen's mother, sister, aunts, and female cousins.

Then Europe lined up in order of precedence, led off by the three emperors of Russia, Austria, and the Ottoman Empire. Then the Kings of Denmark, Norway, Sweden, Prussia, Bavaria, Saxony, Württemberg, Greece, Sardinia, and the Two Sicilies, or their heirs if they were unable to travel to London themselves. They were followed by carriages with their wives, all in flowing black dresses. The first of these carriages carried the only other reigning queen in Europe, Isabel II of Spain. And on went the procession for over two miles including the various Grand Dukes, Dukes, and Princes who were in attendance, a representation of the armed services of the British Empire and its colonies, and several members of Her Majesty's government.

Vicky found the service oddly uplifting. The Archbishop of Canterbury spoke not of endings, but of transitions. While one chapter of Britannia's history closes, another begins. This began the new queen to start thinking about ways she could help move the country forward. She remembered the seediness of the East End where she was held captive and was determined to find ways to help those poor people, and all of the others throughout the kingdom. She knew

Ireland was in particular need, as were all Catholics. They needed recognition, not the repression they have been receiving for so long.

The burial was private and limited to the family only. They took the coffin by train to Windsor where Queen Victoria was interred in the Royal Mausoleum next to her beloved Albert.

***

Nearly thirteen months later, Vicky returned to Westminster Abbey. This time she was four months pregnant and walking in procession towards the Coronation Throne. During all the pomp and circumstance that had changed very little since the time of Edward of Confessor, his Crown was placed on her head and she was anointed with holy oil. She left the Abbey finally and officially Queen Victoria II.

EPILOGUE
1892

"Are you sure you have packed everything we will need?"

"Yes, Vicky, for the forty-seventh time."

"Oh, Louie, don't exaggerate. I'm sure it has not been more than twenty," Vicky teased. This little ritual has become a hallmark of anytime the queen had to travel. Louie, now the Mistress of the Robes and, by marriage, the Marchioness of Salisbury, remained with Vicky after her ascension to the Throne. But now, not only did she have to get the queen ready to go, she also coordinated with the servants who had to pack up the queen's three youngest children. Thankfully, the eldest four all had their own households to worry about them.

One of the challenges of this trip was how to pack for Russia's climate. One always thinks of St. Petersburg as a city of ice and snow. Yet, this trip was taking place in the summer, when even it would be warm to some degree. Though even in July, their warmest month, she had been advised their average temperature was only 23 degrees Celsius with still chilly evenings.

There were also all the extras they were taking this time for the wedding to consider. Vicky's third daughter, Princess Alice, was engaged to the Tsarevich. This trip was to attend their marriage. *No, not Alice*, Louie corrected herself. *It was now Alexandra*. Upon entering the Orthodox religion, the princess was rechristened Alexandra Feodorovna, a process common to all non-Russians who marry into the Imperial Family.

As she looked around at all of the trunks waiting to be moved by the porters, she reflected on the previous times they had been through this. Alice, or rather Alexandra, was the third of Vicky's and Billy's children to marry. The first had been their eldest daughter, Louise, the Princess Royal. Her marriage could almost have been foretold before she was even born. The close friendship between Vicky and the future German Emperor Frederick III could have turned into a marriage itself had they not both been heirs to their respective thrones. It was little wonder that two of their children completed that marital knot. Louise, now German Empress herself, has not had an easy time of it, though. When she married, her husband, Fritz, was only second in line to the throne. But then the fateful year of 1888 saw the death of two German Emperors, first her grandfather-in-law, and three months later, her father-in-law, leaving her and Fritz Jr., now Frederick IV, on the throne. She will not be able to attend the wedding in St. Petersburg as she expects her fourth child in about two months. After three sons, she sorely wishes for a little girl.

Her younger sister, Princess Anne, has had an easier time of it. She has been Crown Princess of Greece for these past three years and already performed her primary duty of providing a son for the next generation. Athens was a beautiful place to have the wedding, evening if a tad warm for Louie's taste.

It was at Anne's wedding that Alice had met the Tsarevich. Anne's mother-in-law was also a Romanoff, a cousin of the current Tsar. Tsarevich Nicholas represented his father at the wedding. He and Alice were immediately smitten. She talked of no one else afterwards and maintained a constant correspondence with him after returning home. Nicholas even traveled all the way to England to visit her, and ultimately propose. After her instruction in Orthodoxy, she converted and the engagement was made public. Now they were all off to St. Petersburg, for better or worse.

Louie knew Vicky was not completely happy with this match. Russia always seems like a country built on a powder keg, ready to blow at any moment. Even the reason it was Nicholas and not his father, Alexander III, who went to Athens was because the Tsar dared not leave the capitol because of demonstrations. Just four years ago, anarchists tried to murder the Imperial Family in their train. It was only the immense physical strength of Alexander that permitted them to survive. And that came only three years after they successfully assassinated his father, Alexander II.

Of Vicky's other children, the Prince of Wales, named William for his father and called Wils by the family, is likely going to be hardest to tie down to the stability of matrimony. He is both the best of and worst of his ancestry. While he has all the inquisitiveness of his mother, he seems to have inherited some of the Hanoverian traits as well. He cannot seem to focus on any one task for any length of time. He often starts projects, gathers experts on the topic to assist, then pass it off to them to follow through. This jumping from one to another would also describe his love life to date. Louie has lost track of the number of times he has been in love. But now, at the age of 31, he does need to be finding someone to settle down with and start a family.

Thankfully, there is a backup plan if he does not manage to do this. His next younger brother, Albert, is engaged to the very sensible Princess May of Teck. May's mother is Queen Victoria I's cousin, Mary of Cambridge, who married the Duke of Teck. Princess May probably gets her no-nonsense practicality from her mother. The family has always been thankful to her for having the presence of mind in the aftermath of the late Queen's death to see to all their guests and make the arrangements for them to stay in London for the funeral.

This leaves the two youngest children, Edward and Beatrice. Edward, currently away at university, is very sensitive and artistic. While it is customary for the royal sons to attend military training, Louie had a hard time seeing that path for Eddy. And Bea, now 16, seems to want to be a bird and simply fly away. She is always more interested in the exotic and distant than anything right here under her nose.

Of course, there have also been the losses since Vicky was crowned. A year later, her grandmother, the Duchess of Kent, died peacefully in her sleep, and was followed a few years later by her step-father, the Duke of Edinburgh. John Brown, never one to really fit in the royal mold, moved back to Scotland after Queen Victoria's death. He never remarried.

The hardest loss came in 1870. The worse part was they family watched it coming for seven years and could nothing to prevent it. Little Prince George was discovered to suffer from hemophilia a few months after his birth. While Vicky did everything she could to try to keep him safe, he was a typical little boy, into everything. Even though he was not permitted to ride a bicycle, this did not prevent him from "borrowing" his elder brother's for a spin from time to time. On one such occasion, he fell over an embankment with it. The internal bleeding proved fatal.

The doctors have warned Vicky and her family that this illness is hereditary and is passed through the women but affects their male children. Thankfully, it seems to affect fewer sons than not. So far, all of Vicky's grandsons appear to be clear of it. However, as the family continues to grow, it will be up to God to decide their ultimate fate.

THE END

HISTORICAL NOTES

In alternate history, it is important to distinguish what really happened from what happened in the world we create.

In the actual timeline, Prince Albert lived until 1861, when he died of illness, not assassination. He and Queen Victoria had nine children, eight of whom had children of their own. Even the one childless daughter lived a full life and married. She simply had the misfortune to marry a homosexual, likely prompting the childlessness.

Their children were:

1. Vicky, married the future German Emperor Frederick III, became mother of Wilhelm II. The Greek Royal Family descends from her daughter.
2. Albert Edward, called Bertie, later Edward VII.
3. Alice, married the Grand Duke of Hesse. Her daughter became Empress Alexandra of Russia
4. Alfred, succeeded as Duke of Saxe-Coburg, had 4 daughters. The Romanian, Serbian, and

current Russian royal families descend from them.

5. Helena, married a Prince of Schleswig-Holstein and had several children but no surviving descendants today.
6. Louise, married – no children.
7. Arthur, Duke of Connaught – the Swedish royal family descends from his daughter.
8. Leopold, Duke of Albany, hemophiliac but married and left two kids before dying rather young.
9. Beatrice, Victoria's caretaker and ancestress of the Spanish royal family

There were indeed several attempts on the Queen's life, but most were carried out by mentally disabled people who often did not even load their weapons. The more serious efforts were thwarted by her protection officers and without injury.

The relationships between Victoria, her mother, and her other relatives is more or less true, with perhaps a little literary license taken in places. Also all of the attendees of the Brussels wedding were real people living at that time, but whether they were at that wedding or not is not known.

Niko was a real person, but any resemblance between the real one and the one in this story is purely coincidental except that he did ultimately marry a commoner morganatically. It is also true that there was a real shortage of princes of an appropriate age for Vicky. In real life, she fell in love with and married Fritz of Prussia, who was really the only available option anyway. Even he was nine years her senior.

Billy Saint Albans was a real person, but again, any resemblance between him and the character in this book is purely coincidental, except that his sisters, mother, and step-father were also the same as those in real life. The real Dukes of Buccleuch, Grafton, Saint Albans, and Richmond were all really male-line descendants of Charles II and his various mistresses.

Lady Louisa Howard (Louie) is a fictional character, but her purported aunt, the Duchess of Sutherland was real. In real life, the Duchess was Mistress of the Robes on and off, depending which party was in power in the government. Also the Duchess of Buccleuch was an early Mistress of the Robes to a young Queen Victoria and they remained close friends until the Duchess' death. The niece that Buccleuch wrote to at the beginning of the story was her niece in real life and the family relations mentioned in the letter were all true.

John Brown was a real person. He did become a very trusted servant to Queen Victoria, some believe they even had an affair. The circumstances how he came to be the servant was changed for the book since in real life Osborne House came to be a royal possession when Albert bought it for Victoria as a present. In this book he never had the chance to do that. In this story John enters royal service a lot earlier than in reality.

In reality, Queen Victoria lived on to January 1901 and was succeeded by her eldest son, Edward VII. Vicky died seven months later of cancer. She was too ill to attend her mother's funeral. For the purposes of the future novels of this series, the real death dates for Vicky (1901) and Billy (1898) will be maintained.

Any other foreign royals mentioned throughout the story really were living at the time suggested.

Princess Vicky was never kidnapped and John Stockley is a completely fictional character. After Prince Albert's death, the Queen did become a bit of a recluse, but not quite to the severe extent as portrayed here. There were public outcries for her to either abdicate or make the Prince of Wales regent, but they were from a reasonably small minority.

The children of Vicky and Billy are completely made up, but care was taken to repair as much of the genealogical damage as possible caused by removing Queen Victoria's eight younger children. The people they marry are all true to history, except Frederick IV of Germany. He is replacing the historical Wilhelm II. These children and their descendants will be primary characters in the remainder of this series.

Finally, all the of the government officials portrayed herein were in the same offices at the same times indicated. The same is true for Dr. Snow, although Mrs. Sutton is a fictional character.

SNEAK PEEK
Book 2: The Children of Victoria II

Buckingham Palace
1 July 1914

I.M.K. Die Kaiserin
Neuer Stadtschloss
Berlin

Dearest Lulu,

The past 3 days have been quite the whirlwind, but I think it's all sorted now. Fritzi and I are in complete agreement that neither of our kingdoms have any business getting involved with Austria's problems. We have both implored Nicky to stay out of it too, but he's convinced he is bound by treaty to those Serbians. And now he is committed by blood, as I have been informed the first shots of this war have been fired between Austrian and Russian soldiers...in Budapest of all places!

Thank God! the French and Italians have agreed to stay out of it was well. But of course the French aren't going anywhere without Big Brother Britain there to hold their hand. I only hope Italy can stay out, what with being so close to the conflict. It wouldn't take much for the fighting to enter their territory. But Victor Emanuel does not want to fight, so that will go a long way to keeping the cooler heads there.

It is all quite mad. But then so is the murder of the Archduke in Sarajevo which sparked all of this. It is a real shame. I had so much hope for him to pull Austro-Hungary into this century, something old Franz Joseph is just not capable of.

It's even more a shame they couldn't stop there but also shot his charming wife, those dogs! She wasn't even equal, she had no role in the political situation whatsoever. Such a loss. She was so gracious when they visited London a few years ago, you would never know she was not born to a royal house. There's another area, maintaining such strict rules about equal birth, where Franz Joseph lives too much in the past.

But then, maybe so does Fritzi? Have they settled the matter of Willy's fiancée? So what that her father is a Count and not a King? When I met them at Viktoria Luise's wedding, she fit in just as well as any princess would, and maybe a mite better than Alexandra has, if I'm being perfectly honest. The point is she makes the boy happy. Is that not good enough? If Papa was good enough for Mama, then Ina-Maria should be good enough for Willy. He's not the heir or anything, so let him be happy!

In happier news, London has grown hot sooner than usual this year. Thankfully, we seem to have our end of the continent settled so I can escape to Windsor for a few weeks. Might do a little fishing while I'm there.

My love to the kids and give an extra kiss to
those grandbabies from their Grossonkel Wils!

William R.

William V, King of the United Kingdom of Great Britain and
Ireland and so forth, sat back in his chair after finishing his
letter to his favorite sister, Louise, now the German
Empress. To each other they were still Wils and Lulu, those
same kids who chased each other around Buckingham
Palace with the brother, Bertie.

Wils missed those simpler times. Mama spend much of
the day sequestered in her office, going through "her boxes."
Papa would romp with them in the nursery until the tutors
showed up. Initially, it was just him, Bertie, and Lulu. The
others got old enough to romp with them too, Annie, Alix,
Eddy, and finally baby Bea. But they were just young enough
to feel not quite the same generation as Wils and Bertie. It
was Lulu, the number three child, who bridged that gap. Of
course, there was also poor Georgie, right in the middle, but
he could never play with him.

Georgie was the first time Wils experienced death. At
ten years old, he had a hard time understanding it. All he
knew was his youngest brother was gone. Not that he had
been there much anyway. They kept him locked away like a
valuable porcelain doll, and he was just as fragile. At times,
Wils wishes he was still the innocent child who had never
heard of hemophilia before.

Now, each new baby, the family holds its collective
breath, and hopes the child will not be infected. Even though
the doctors assured him the disease was passed through the
female line only, he still prayed heavier than at any other
time in his life when his own son was born. Of course, young
Prince George was clear.

Lulu had been exceptionally lucky as well, her boys
were all healthy. Of course now the worrying starts again

with her daughter, Viktoria Luise. She is just starting her own family. Little Ernie is only four months old. He appears to be okay so far, but the concern is still there, both for him and the future children she has.

Then there is Alix, now the Tsarina of Russia. The family blood curse has found a new home in her little boy, Alexei. But he has made it this far, twice as far as Georgie did. There will be big celebrations in St. Petersburg for his 10th birthday in a couple of weeks. Wils hoped the boy will be able to get out and enjoy it all. At least he has four older sisters to help keep him safe.

If only they had done the same for Georgie, Wils thought, a self-condemnation he placed on himself, Bertie, and Lulu daily now for 44 years.

ABOUT THE AUTHOR

Daniel A. Willis writes both fiction and nonfiction. Through his nonfiction work, he has been established as one of the foremost authorities on post-Napoleonic European royal families.

He publishes two annually updated reference books: *The Reporters Guide to the Royal Families of Europe* and *The Complete Line of Succession*.

His previous works include genealogies of the descendants of King George I of Great Britain, Empress Maria Theresia, and King Louis XIII of France, as well as current family biographies of the Habsburgs and the Romanoffs.

As a fiction writer he puts his historical knowledge to great use by weaving history with fantasy. His *Immortal Series* inserts near-immortal beings into such historical events as the murder of Rasputin in Russia and the Sand Creek massacre in Colorado.

A native of Ohio, Mr. Willis has called Denver home for more than three decades.

OTHER EXQUISITE FICTION FROM
D. X. VAROS, LTD.

CPSIA information can be obtained
at www.ICGtesting.com
Printed in the USA
LVHW020220130421
684331LV00005B/105